RISE OF THE
ANOINTED

BOOK ONE

JASON C. JOYNER

LAUNCH

D1065964

little lamb
BOOKS

Launch
Text copyright © 2018 Jason C. Joyner
ISBN: 978-0-9986243-8-9 (Paperback)
Library of Congress Control Number: 2018939839

Published by Little Lamb Books
www.littlelambbooks.com
P.O. Box 211724, Bedford, TX 76021

Scriptures taken from the Holy Bible, New International Version, NIV.
Copyright ©1973, 1978, 1984, 2011 by Biblica, Inc. Used by permission of
Zondervan. All rights reserved worldwide. *www.zondervan.com*
The NIV and New International Version are trademarks registered in the
United States Patent and Trademark Office by Biblica, Inc.

The characters and events in this book are fictional, and any resemblance to
actual persons, living or dead, or events is coincidental.

Written by Jason C. Joyner, *jasoncjoyner.com*
Edited by Lindsay Schlegel, *lindsayschlegel.com*
Cover design by TLC Book Design, *TLCBookDesign.com*
Interior design by Marisa Jackson for TLC Book Design

First Edition
Printed in Canada

TO MOM,

who gave me
the love of reading
and so much more,

AND TO DAD,

who left me
with a good legacy

CHARACTER KEY

Demarcus Bartlett: A 16-year-old African-American teenager originally from San Diego, who recently moved to San Jose with his single mother. Demarcus is a strong leader with potential and looks at the Launch Conference as an opportunity to make his mom proud.

Lily Beausoliel: A 16-year-old who moved from Redmond, Washington, a year ago when her father got a new job in Palo Alto, California. She lost family members in a car accident and has been battling grief. For her, the Launch Conference is a fresh start.

Harry Wales: A 16-year-old originally from Kalispell, Montana, who moved to the Bay Area with his parents when his lumberjack father decided to switch careers. His mother, originally from England, thought it appropriate to name him Harry with his red hair.

Sarah Jane Langely: A quiet 17-year-old, originally from Phoenix, Arizona, who lives with her parents and younger brother. She has dealt with bullying and is confused about why she was picked to attend the Launch Conference.

Rosa Gonzalez: An 18-year-old who just graduated high school and was invited to the Launch Conference. She has a tough attitude and a hard time connecting with anyone for any length of time.

Missy Austin: Classmate of Lily's at her private school. Orginally friends, Missy unfriended Lily and now treats her like garbage.

Iaonnes/John: A mysterious older man keeping an eye on the Alturas Collective and the Launch Conference. As a custodian, he's on the look-out for those who will heed his warnings and take action to stop the impending danger.

Kelsey: Simon's assistant. She follows his directions without questioning his motives or his plans.

Simon Mazor: Influential tech genius and the country's youngest billionaire. He founded Alturas and started the Flare network. Simon hosts the Launch Conference in order to find the girl of light and move forward with his hidden agenda of impacting youth globally.

PART
1

Chapter One

This might not be a great idea, but Demarcus Bartlett had to see if he could outrace a sports car.

He crouched behind a bush next to the on-ramp for the highway. His blue hoodie concealed his shoulder-length dreads, so it should be hard for any cars passing by on Santa Clara Street to see him. No Toyotas or Hondas would do. His prize would have some horses under the hood. He'd have to be patient. Not many cars out at 5 A.M. would fit his needs.

He checked his shoelaces again, his fingers fumbling over the knots. Didn't want to trip at highway speeds. That could get ugly. He glanced at his phone again. He had a job to go to, but the drive to see what he was capable of overwhelmed him.

Even with the risk of being discovered.

The light for the on-ramp turned red. In the soft rosy glow, a growling beast stopped at the white line. Its shiny black paint reflected the traffic light off of the hood. A rev of the Camaro's engine. The owner was ready to try out his toy as well. The blinker flicked on, signaling a turn onto Highway 101.

This guy was the one.

Demarcus wiped his palms on his hoodie again and shook them out like a runner at the starter's gate. His heart leapt at the thought of going through with this.

Mr. Camaro would blow right by his hiding place. A smile stretched across Demarcus's face. *Here's hoping this guy knows how to use the accelerator.*

Green light cut through the darkness, and the black car jumped forward, turning onto the ramp and surging by him. Demarcus gave him a few seconds' head start to make it fair as he noted the time to track his speed.

Three. Two. One.

He took off from his sprinter's stance and pumped his arms and legs. Up the concrete ramp he raced. The spring California air chilled him as he took after his target. His hood slipped off, dreads trailing in his wake.

The roar of the muscle car carried through the early morning silence. That guy wanted to open it up, and in minimal traffic, this was the perfect place to do it. Demarcus thanked the man while he puffed air in and out to fuel his muscles.

The taillights grew closer.

The Camaro blew by a semi. Demarcus passed the same truck a couple of seconds later. How fast was he going? If only his cell phone had a speedometer app.

His senses heightened as well: he spied an obstacle approaching fast, and he dodged a fallen muffler on the side of the road. His eyes watered from the wind whipping by. *Maybe I need some shades when I do this.*

The Camaro seemed to slow, but Demarcus knew it was only an illusion.

He'd caught it.

He ran alongside the streaking vehicle and let up for a moment to keep pace, glancing over to see the driver's face. The guy didn't realize that a teenager was zipping alongside him.

A laugh broke through Demarcus's breaths as he gave an extra surge.

Now the Camaro tasted his dust.

He ran for another couple of minutes until he found an exit. A black kid walking along a highway would probably attract attention, so he needed to stop in a reasonable area. He followed the curve around to a suburb he didn't recognize. His trip had taken him north past Fremont. Not his usual stomping grounds.

His shoes skidded to a stop. As the sensation of wind blowing by him subsided, he pulled his phone out and checked the timer. Ten minutes had passed. The sign said Union City. He'd traveled twenty miles in that time. What did that work out to for speed?

One hundred twenty miles per hour.

Demarcus pumped his fist in the air as adrenaline rushed through his body. He'd run faster than a cheetah. Faster than a Camaro. His lungs didn't complain at all.

The most insane part? He couldn't quite access it yet, but he could feel more within him.

Exercise. He'd work out and build things up even more. Wind sprints back and forth at the old abandoned warehouse where no one would wonder about a sixteen-year-old dashing around at impossible speeds.

A scent wafted into his nostrils. The pungent odor of burnt rubber irritated his nose. Where was that coming from?

He lifted a foot and gawked at the worn tread on his new sneakers. Apparently running shoes weren't made for triple-digit speed. This made it three pairs in two months. Highway speeds must wear them out faster. He poked the tread. They'd last a little longer.

Shoot, what time is it? He hadn't checked that when he stopped his timer. The screen read 5:15.

Time to get to work. He'd gotten up this early to deliver newspapers. It had taken a lot of arguing to get his mom to agree to it. She didn't want her special boy in harm's way, yet she also appreciated his motivation to earn some bank on his own.

He clenched a fist, thinking of how challenging things had been before the move to Silicon Valley. Until Mama had finished school and gotten her job, they had struggled to keep up with the rent and the basics. Finances were improving, but the cost of starting over had been a big deal. He had to help out somehow. Besides, how else would he keep up with his new need of quality footwear?

Delivering the papers didn't take long. Making sure they didn't break patio decorations was the challenge. His boss couldn't believe it when Demarcus asked for another two routes. Hey, what were another few minutes?

He stretched his legs a couple of times to keep the machine loose. His grin wouldn't subside at his thoughts of dashing about so fast. He didn't know why God let him do this, but he was thankful for every blessing. If only he could share this with someone!

Eh, that probably wasn't the best idea right now. Visions of men in bubble suits probing him with needles freaked him out.

On the return trip to Santa Clara County there was more traffic. The early birds had begun their commutes, but it wasn't too bad for California standards. Again, no one seemed to notice him as he skimmed the edge of the road.

It took him fifteen minutes to backtrack due to his slower pace—just a leisurely jog past all the normal people in their Corollas.

What did this mean? The last several weeks weren't dreams or hallucinations. His impromptu race this morning proved it. He looked to the sky.

"God, I'm so grateful, but I'd also like a hint of what I'm supposed to do now."

Demarcus knew the source of his gift had to be divine. Why him? What did the Lord have in mind for a kid just scraping by?

The exit for his city had a windier road. It felt like his personal roller coaster. He couldn't help releasing a whoop gliding into south San Jose.

Now, off to Parkland Avenue and his routes. He'd finish in ten minutes and head home to get ready for another day at school. If he was lucky, Mama would have a plate of her cinnamon apple French toast ready for him.

Skirting the park, he almost tripped over a branch sticking out from behind a bush near the sidewalk. He hopped to the side and hit the brakes. Even if most people wouldn't hit the branch at high speed, he didn't want them to trip over it.

Of course, it took him twenty yards to stop. He jogged back over. And recoiled.

It wasn't a stick. A pair of legs lay sprawled out on the cement.

Chapter Two

"Lily? Come on. You're going to be late."

Lily Beausoliel groaned as she put the last touches on her hair. *Here we go again.*

Her stepmom, Kelly, thought people were late if they weren't ten minutes early. What did it matter? Lily didn't care about getting to class on time anymore. If the universe intended to treat her like it had over the last year, nothing really mattered.

Her thrift store boots sat by her closet door. She grabbed them and her backpack and trudged down the stairs. She tossed the pack next to the table and it landed with a thud. All the stupid books from her elite private school echoed against the hardwood floor.

Kelly jerked around at the sound and dropped a butter knife. At least that brought a smile to Lily's face.

"You can't scare me like that. You know I jump easy. Now hurry up and get those … *things* on. You'll have to eat on the way to Everett. If only you—"

The stepmonster must have noticed Lily's hair.

"What did you do? Your beautiful blonde hair! You dyed it black!"

Lily plopped into the kitchen chair and started lacing up her boots. The dress code called for a white blouse and a plaid skirt down to her knees, but her worn leather army boots would be an expression of her mood. Along with the midnight color of her hair.

Kelly fingered a long dark strand of Lily's hair, clucking her tongue. "Your father is going to have a fit when he returns from his trip. What am I supposed to tell him?" Her face crinkled up like a Shar Pei's.

It probably wouldn't matter, honestly. Lily doubted if he would even notice. She shrugged. "He'll have to get used to it."

"Ugh. What am I going to do with you? Just … hurry to the car. We've got to go. Do you want some bran toast?"

Lily grabbed a S'mores-flavored Pop-Tart. "Nah, I'm good. Thanks for taking me."

She couldn't identify much good in her life right now, and while spending more time with her stepmom didn't thrill her, it beat the carpool with the catty Hot Tops—the main clique at Everett Academy. She'd given up that privilege a few months ago.

Silence filled the car on the way to school. Kelly opened her mouth to say something a couple of times, but Lily wielded her cold shoulder to devastating effect. Once when she caught Kelly glancing her way, a twang of guilt hit. Kelly wasn't the source of her trials. Just a symptom.

Lily was done bleeding for everyone. Extending a peace offering wasn't going to happen today.

They pulled into the half-circle drive to the posh campus, and Lily hopped out, muttering goodbye as she exited Kelly's BMW. She ducked through a spring drizzle into the main doors. At least the weather agreed with her mood.

After pushing through the hallway logjam, she slipped into theater class with a sigh. At the start of the school year she'd been excited to take it. Now the class just served as a cruel reminder of how fast things could change.

A smile illuminated Clara Casper's scarred face as she pat the open seat in the back of the room, next to the window. Lily cringed at how well her friend had dealt with an awful situation, especially compared to Lily's brooding. The ugliness of her own attitude bubbled up like bile in her throat.

"I think we get to do our first walk-through on the stage today. I can't wait." Clara bounced in her chair like an excited puppy. "Hey, I like what you did with your hair. Did you do it for the play?"

That would make a good cover story. "Yeah. I wanted to really get myself into the part."

Missy Austin, the queen of the Hot Tops, walked by them. If there was one person Lily couldn't stand, it was her former friend. Missy looked down on the two of them with her nose wrinkled. "Wow, Lily. With that hair you almost match Clara for the freak section."

Betrayal stabbed her heart again. The insults made each day in this class torture. Lily usually weathered the storm, but she couldn't let Missy get away with hurting her friend.

She stood in Missy's way, only coming to her chin. "Look, cupcake. You might think you're all sweet on the outside. Let me tell you, you're rotten on the inside. Go sit down with the rest of your garbage."

Missy's eyes bulged and she fumbled for a response. Before she could wield her tongue, Mr. Barton called for everyone to sit down.

Missy moved up front. Lily waited a moment then sat down by Clara, who took her hand and gave it a squeeze. "Thanks for being there for me. No one sees me through my scar, except you."

Clara had survived a house fire years ago. As a consequence, she'd sustained burns on the left side of her face. The corner of her lip permanently turned up in a smile, still, Clara had such a joy that the other side usually matched. Lily didn't care about much right now, but she'd fight for Clara—a friend who gave Lily hope in her own darkness.

She watched Missy glance back and whisper to her group of crones. Missy was the first person to welcome Lily at this school, after her father's impulse move from Washington. And now, just a few months later, Missy couldn't stand the sight of Lily. And vice versa.

Mr. Barton slid in front of his desk in his old Birkenstock sandals. Lily always wondered if they were relics from Woodstock. He smiled and patiently stroked his curly beard while waiting for the chatter to subside.

"This week we're going to begin walk-throughs on the spring play. Let's go into the auditorium and start doing our blocking."

Lily followed at the end of the line as everyone filed through the door that led to backstage. Clusters of kids congregated on the stage. The Hot Tops in the class occupied center stage. So fitting.

Lily and Clara nestled into a spot near the curtain, next to a stand with a large spotlight on it. Lily wanted to stay away from Missy before Lily did something she'd regret.

Mr. Barton waved his arms in the air and whistled to get their attention. "Okay, ladies and gentlemen. Our performance of *You Can't Take It With You* opens in two weeks. We've been working on our lines and characterization. Now it's time to put everything together. Clear the middle of the stage, and we'll set up how it will be for real."

Mr. Barton directed traffic and motioned for Missy's crew to move. They shuffled over toward Lily's spot, and she narrowed her eyes, trying to give off her best back-off vibe. Clara twirled past Lily in a bout of her endless enthusiasm.

"I've been working on my ballet twirls for my character. How does it look?"

Clara spun right in front of Missy and stepped on her foot. Missy jerked away even though the contact was mild.

"Get off me, you clumsy troll." Missy shoved Clara into the light stand, knocking her to the ground.

That was it.

Lily cocked her fist ready to pound Missy's prissy nose when her eye caught movement in her peripheral vision. The spotlight was tipping, and Clara lay right under it. The huge metal canister plummeted toward her.

Lily thrust her hands toward it, and brilliant light flashed. "No!"

Chapter Three

Demarcus bent down and stared at the body in front of him—a man with a scraggly beard and wild tufts of grey hair sticking out of his head. Splotches of dirt stained the front of his tropical-print shirt, and grime lined each nail of the one hand Demarcus could see.

Was the dude dead? Demarcus recovered from his initial shock enough to lean in. What was the way to check? Look, listen, feel. Something like that.

He pressed his ear to the man's chest and looked at his face. He felt the man's ribs rise, and at the same time, a blast of alcohol-laced breath hit his nose. Okay, the guy was alive. Stinky, but alive.

A homeless guy, maybe? The man lay on his side, one arm askew above his head. Demarcus rolled the man onto his back, thinking it might make him more comfortable. That's when he noticed a trail of dried blood from the man's scalp running down the other side of his face.

The man wasn't breathing very fast. Demarcus's fingers searched for a pulse on the man's neck. Very faint, from what he could tell.

He'd better call 911. He pulled his phone out to dial. Before Demarcus could swipe the screen, the man started convulsing. His body shook and a frothy substance spilled from his mouth.

Demarcus recoiled. This dude was going to die right in front of him. No way would an ambulance make it in time.

He glanced around. The street was deserted in the early morning hour.

But he could.

He stooped down and pulled the man to a sitting position. With one knee down, Demarcus managed to wrestle him up and sling him over his shoulder, despite the man's quaking.

Okay, where was the hospital? He was a block from Parkland, so St. Matthew's would be a couple of miles away. Now the test was how fast could he go carrying an adult.

His legs churned like pistons against the sidewalk, propelling him forward. The extra weight challenged him, and even using the fireman technique, the body threw off his balance. He struggled to keep steady, and it affected his momentum.

The homeless man gurgled and twitched.

Push it, Demarcus. He's not going to last much longer. He leaned in, willing his legs to move faster. His mouth dried out with the stress.

A crosswalk signal changed to red, and a truck turned right in front of him. Demarcus grabbed onto the man tighter. He planted a foot to spin. The truck veered by a few inches away as Demarcus finished his turn and squirted past the bumper toward his destination. His eyes stung from the exhaust hanging in the air.

The lights of the hospital windows rose in the skyline in front of him. A couple more blocks. A surge of power emanated from deep within Demarcus. Reserves he didn't know he had flooded over his skin and soaked to his bones. He flew forward, a new gear unlocked.

A ramp led up to the receiving area for the ER. He slowed his pace enough to avoid questions. *Okay, God, thank you for getting me here. Now forgive me if I have to lie a little.*

He paused for the automatic doors. They slid open with a whoosh. A bored female clerk and a police officer over in the corner both looked up at him.

"I need help, here! I found this guy passed out nearby and he started shaking."

A bunch of people in scrubs surrounded him and led him past the check-in desk. An empty gurney rolled forward, and Demarcus laid the stricken man on the bed. A circle of nurses and doctors surrounded the man and barked out orders to stabilize him.

Demarcus didn't know what to do now. Running, he could do. Medicine? *Nuh-huh.* He backed through the ER doors and planned to quietly excuse himself when a woman with red hair cornered him.

"Did you bring that man in?"

Demarcus looked around, but there was no one else to finger. "Yeah, I guess so."

"How did you find him? I need to ask some questions."

The clerk took down notes on what Demarcus could offer about the man he saved. Demarcus glanced at the clock on the wall. Great. Even with his speed, he'd have to push it to get his routes done before school. If he arrived late he'd hear it from his mom. Would school take an excuse note about saving someone's life?

"Now I need your contact information if we have more questions, or if the police have any questions."

"You need to get a hold of me? And what do the police have to do with this?"

"Sometimes we need more data afterward, and law enforcement may get involved." The clerk looked down at her clipboard. "What's your name and address?"

Before he could answer, he noticed the police officer walking up in his peripheral vision. *Great. What kind of attention am I going to get now?*

Demarcus turned to face the officer, ignoring the last question of the clerk. "Can I help you, sir?

The name tag read Maldonado. "That was a good thing you did. What I would like to know is what you were doing out at this hour."

Scenarios juggled in Demarcus's mind as he considered how to answer. He clicked his tongue and drew in a breath. "Just delivering the newspaper." Probably best to leave out the part about drag-racing on foot.

"So, where's your papers?"

"I left them outside."

The officer raised an eyebrow. "You mean you stopped before the door to leave them, while carrying a sick man on your back?"

Mama's admonition to keep it polite and open, especially with dealing with authority figures, screamed in his mind.

"I'll go get them and show you, if you'd like."

The clerk glanced at the officer and took the hint—she could get her information later. The officer nodded. "Sure thing. Don't take off. I'll be watching you."

Demarcus turned without showing any emotion and strode through the sliding door. He wasn't prepared for the officer calling him on the papers. The trouble he landed in just for helping a person in need! Panic momentarily fluttered through his gut.

Sorry, Lord, for the lie. And forgive me for what I have to do now.

Demarcus walked just past the view of the doors, checked his surroundings, and made a beeline for his newspaper route, hoping that the officer would have something better to investigate other than a random black kid doing a good deed.

Chapter Four

Lily's heart resumed beating as everyone shouted. The auditorium erupted in chaos.

Missy gaped and waved her hands at her eyes, all the while claiming the push was an accident. Mr. Barton barged his way through students to get to the point of impact.

Clara curled up into a ball, her arms covering her head for protection. The spotlight lay crumpled in a heap a foot away from her, smoke rising from the canister.

Lily rubbed her throbbing temples as she tried to comprehend what happened. The light must've blown on its way down, and the force knocked it away from her friend. That was the only explanation.

She had screamed and raised her arms out to knock the metal canister out of the way, then a white light flashed as the stand fell. Maybe she had hit it. Her hands tingled like they were asleep.

Although, the tingling had been happening more often lately.

Mr. Barton knelt next to Clara. "Are you okay? Does anything hurt?"

She slowly unfurled and checked her arms and legs. She shook them all for good measure. "I think I'm good, Mr. Barton. As long as it doesn't involve open flames, I'm ducky."

He helped Clara up. Lily stepped close to get in his field of vision. "Mr. Barton, Missy pushed her into the tripod, and that caused the thing to tip over. It was no accident."

Missy shot a look of innocence at Mr. Barton. "I did *not* push her. I just put my hands up to keep her from running into me. I swear."

Kids bickered over what really happened. Lily fumed at the bully's obvious lies. It would feel really good to knock some of those perfect teeth loose. She couldn't believe they'd once been friends.

Before Lily got the chance to do something she might regret, Mr. Barton corralled everyone into the house seats to calm down and doing some "centering" exercises. Lily glanced at her goofy friend as Clara focused her breathing and gamely went along with the rest of the class. Justice was delayed, but if Lily could help it, Missy wouldn't get away with anything.

Lily closed her eyes so she wouldn't get caught glaring at Missy and concentrated on shaking her hands out, trying to get the feeling in her fingers to return.

The rest of the day droned on. Thankfully. She didn't need the excitement of drama class to repeat itself. Lily noticed a few people giving her funny looks toward the end of the day, the only thing that appeared unusual.

Ugh. Let 'em stare.

All she wanted to do was get her homework over with and shut the world out with her headphones and laptop. Maybe she could find some solace playing with pictures if she could get her editing software to cooperate. Clara met her at the stairs and hugged her before they hit the main doors.

The morning clouds had broken, and the California rays bathed Lily in warmth. She took a deep breath and savored the feeling. After the stressful day, the sun felt especially bright and cheerful. Not quite enough to clear her internal storms, but it calmed them.

Clara spied her ride and waved goodbye, bounding down the curved ramp to the main sidewalk. Lily softened her frown at Clara's energy. The girl survived another near disaster and appeared none the worse for wear.

Lily leaned against a white colonnade and scanned the parking lot. She wondered where Kelly was. Out of character for her to be late. Lily was ready to get out of here. Especially when she heard snickering behind her.

"Who do you pay to do your hair? You should fire them for the mess they made of it." She knew Missy's condescending tone anywhere.

Lily whirled around and snarled, "What's your problem? Black not your color? Well, it should be—it matches your heart."

The pack of girls pointed at Lily's head, and Missy giggled. "She doesn't even know how bad it looks."

Laughter followed her as Lily stomped out to the parking lot. Kelly pulled up just in time. Lily ripped the back door open, threw her backpack across the bench, and plopped inside the front seat.

"How was your day, honey?"

"Awful. Can we just go home?" *Before the tears start.*

Kelly didn't answer. When Lily looked at her, Kelly was gawking at her hair. "What?"

"Sweetheart, can you decide on a look and stick with it?"

Lily shook her head, confused. *What is everyone babbling about?* She yanked the sun visor down and checked out her reflection. Her jaw dropped.

Only the last half of her long hair was black. The rest had turned back to shiny yellow.

Chapter Five

Demarcus slipped in through the kitchen door, worn out from a long, dragging day at school. He wanted to hole up and do more research on how to test his speed.

First, some fuel. As he reached for the fridge door, he heard conversation from the living room. His mama and a strange voice. Who was here?

A man's voice carried past the door. "What time does Demarcus get home from school?" Paranoia jolted through his chest. Was he caught by the police for this morning? The question of security cameras or other ways to ID him had nagged him all day.

Demarcus snatched a banana off the counter to satisfy his rising hunger and crept up the wooden staircase. Hopefully he could avoid any unwanted entanglements.

A loud creak reverberated from the fifth step.

Dang. That one was the trap.

"Dee, are you home?" Mama's voice carried through the hallway. With the voice of a gospel singer, there was no mistaking when Mama called.

"Yes, ma'am."

"I need you in the living room, please."

He hung his backpack, steeled himself with a deep breath, and pushed through the swinging door into the living room.

"Hey Mama. How's your day? And who's the strange guy on the couch?"

Whoops. His stream of consciousness ran right out of his mouth. He wasn't expecting to see a dude wearing Chukka boots, rolled up pants, and a button-up shirt under a sweater sipping a glass of lemonade. Total. Hipster.

So he wasn't a cop. Sweet. But who was this guy? Could it still have to do with his racing on the highways? Or with the homeless man at the hospital?

"Demarcus! Where are your manners?"

He hid the banana behind his back as if it were a secret weapon and offered his other hand to the visitor. "I'm so sorry. I wasn't expecting anyone. My name is Demarcus. Pleased to meet you."

The hipster took Demarcus's hand with a weak grip and wiggled his arm, then adjusted his horn-rimmed glasses as he sat down. "I'm glad to meet you, Demarcus. I'm Fredrick Noble. I was just talking to your mom about you."

Demarcus's heart skipped in his chest.

Mama's demeanor seemed normal, though, so that was a good sign.

Demarcus backed toward a floral-patterned chair and sat down, smashing his fruit in the process. He pulled the banana onto his lap and tried to act relaxed, lazily draping an arm over the armrest. "Really? You were talking about me? What's up?"

Fredrick sipped his drink. "Well, Demarcus, I'm with the Alturas Collective. Our company is looking for some bright youth to help us in our global outreach."

Wait, Alturas? As in, Flare? Dee fingered the outline of his phone in his jean pocket. This was trippy. He'd just checked his Flare account before getting off the bus.

Mama poked his leg, jarring him from his mental shock. "Dee, pay attention."

"Sorry. Did you say Alturas?"

Fredrick set his lemonade down and adjusted his cuff. "Yes, I did. We're hosting a conference for gifted individuals a few weeks after school ends. We've been scouting regional schools to find teens with exceptional potential. I was talking to your mother about the possibility of your coming to our gathering in June."

Now this was weird.

"I don't know what to say. I guess one thing is: are you sure you have the right Demarcus Bartlett?" His grades were good, still, he was no genius. Mama made sure he worked hard at homework as the price for doing sports, but he didn't feel like he belonged at some super-smart symposium.

Fredrick chuckled. "I assure you that you're the one we're interested in. If you're wondering, it's not all about grades. It's about potential. Leadership. It's about the ability to make a difference in our world."

Mama leaned over from her sage green couch and squeezed Demarcus's leg. "Isn't this great, Demarcus? I've always said you were special. You have a destiny. God has kept you for a reason. It's time to let your light shine."

His finger traced one of the flowers on the cushion. Was this a coincidence? A few weeks ago, he'd finally gotten out of his walking boot, the result of an ankle fracture. Since then he'd lived the most amazing—and fast—days of his life.

Fredrick flashed a wide, inviting smile. "See, we're interested in people who influence peers, who show leadership, and who can point the way to others. Everyone is concerned about bullying, isolation, and wasting time, especially in cyberspace. Flare holds the center of the social media world. We want to use our influence to transform society. That's why we don't need the best GPA or test scores. We are drawn to potential."

Demarcus absentmindedly peeled his bruised banana and chomped a bite. What kind of opportunity would this be? Could it lift his hard-working mother out of the edge of the suburb into a place she deserved to live?

"Well, what does this conference mean?"

Fredrick slid a glossy multi-page brochure out from a black leather attaché embossed with the symbol for Flare, a torch with swirling lines around it. Boy, that case looked fancy.

Demarcus glanced around their tiny home. The second-hand furniture had never bothered him before. Now the worn upholstery and mismatched décor seemed out of place with this upscale dude.

"Alturas is inviting you to come. It's short notice, we know, so don't worry about the cost. It starts the second week of June, and we hold it in Santa Clara at our main campus. You'll join about fifty other potentials for inspiration sessions over four days. It won't be anything like school. It'll be an experience you'll never forget. You'll brainstorm, bounce ideas off of other gifted peers, and unlock the doors for the next generation."

"Heh." Demarcus eyed him. "Does that mean a lot of texting and make-out sessions?"

Mama gave him that look again, and his shoulders dropped.

Fredrick laughed, then he tapped his watch a few times and focused on Demarcus, his eyes offering a warm acceptance. "Don't worry. There will be plenty of supervision from Alturas's best and brightest. Bringing a bunch of teens together might seem like a bad idea, but we believe in you. How will anything change if those with the keys aren't allowed to start driving?"

Demarcus heard the ticking of the wooden Swiss clock Mama had just found at a yard sale. He watched the second hand flick across the face as he considered Fredrick's offer.

Pride welled up in him. He'd been recognized. For a long time, he was just another kid trying to climb out of a difficult past. Mama's powerful will wouldn't let him settle for gang-bangin' or slacking, so he'd always kept his head up and pushed forward.

This spring was supposed to be his earth-shattering debut on the track team, especially since he was still the new kid at school, only to have it dashed with the freak accident that broke his ankle. Then his gift manifested—only after he couldn't show it off on the field.

Well, what could he hurt in going to this conference?

But would his overprotective mother let him go?

"It sounds cool. What do you think, Mama?"

Demarcus's mother, Mary Bartlett, was a woman full of faith, yet sensible to a fault. She wouldn't get talked into the name brand if there wasn't a real benefit. Demarcus's hopes had been dashed in the past when she didn't go for something because it was the must-have gadget or label. Would she buy this guy's sales pitch?

Her eyes glistened as she gripped a few Kleenex. "I knew when I woke up in the hospital and you looked at me for the first time that you had a purpose. You were born for such a time as this. This must be a gift from God. I'm so excited for you."

She sighed and tilted her head up in a faraway gaze looking off to the horizon. Or at the spider webs he was supposed to have cleaned up in the corner of the living room last weekend.

Mr. Hipster slapped his legs. "Well then, let's talk. I need your personal info, and we'll get the application started."

He handed Demarcus another leather portfolio, this, too stamped with the torch logo of the Alturas Collective. Demarcus crossed his leg onto his opposite knee to give him a base to write.

His mom shook her head and came back to reality, wrinkling her nose. "Do you smell burnt rubber?"

Chapter Six

Lily stared at her reflection in the mirror. What kind of cheap product had she bought? The black in her hair had faded to the last inch or so of her hair. Her light blonde hair had resurfaced, if anything lighter than before. The dye must really be bad if it couldn't even stay in a day.

Except she hadn't bought the generic Walmart brand. It was the most expensive box she could find.

No wonder everyone was laughing at her. She really did look like a freak today.

The last strains of sunlight filtered through the window. Lily jerked the curtains closed and kicked off her skirt, switching to some baggy sweats and a black goth band t-shirt. She tossed her brush onto her nightstand. Instead of landing by her alarm clock, it knocked over her white picture frames.

The frames' dust footprints showed how long it had been since she'd deep-cleaned her room. She picked up the white-framed mementos and wiped her finger over the top. Four smiling people beamed through the glass. Two would never be in her life again.

Luke had a gap in his front teeth and big eyes that shined. Their mom snuggled him close, his floppy brown hair a contrast to his mom's platinum mane. The love was evident in her eyes.

Lily carefully replaced the picture. She could remember the camera settings she'd used to get that picture, and exactly how many times she ran back by her dad when she set the timer.

One year ago. Seemed like an eternity. The raw ache in her gut ate away at her remaining will.

As her eyes started to mist, she turned away. Her homework sat unopened on her desk. One thing she'd held onto was keeping up in class. She wasn't stupid, and her pride kept her from looking that way with bad grades. However, today teetered as a tipping point. Could she keep holding on?

Lily punched her password into her laptop and reached for her wireless headphones to shut out the world, when she heard a soft rap on her door. Kelly must've made an after-school snack to try and break through. It was a common tactic to get Lily out of her room, and it was a nice thought. Not today, though.

Another knock. *Okay, what's going on?* She yanked the door open, ready to shut down the charity act.

"Hey, Kitten."

Jack Beausoliel, her father, stood at the threshold. What was he doing here? Wasn't he supposed to be on another business trip somewhere? She couldn't keep track anymore.

"Hey." She leaned against the doorframe, her features frozen. If she betrayed her emotions, how would she ever rein them in again?

He scratched the back of his neck, his nervous tic when he didn't know what to say. Lily had seen it a lot lately. "Um, I'm glad to see you. Sounds like you had a rough day?"

She fingered her hair with the receding black tips. "Nothing out of the ordinary." *Unless you consider an exploding stage light ordinary.* "Didn't know you were going to be home tonight."

"I got a special call. There's someone downstairs who wants to meet you. Are you … presentable?" He looked at her casual outfit with a raised eyebrow.

No sense getting changed. "Yeah, I'm good. Who is it?"

"You'll see."

He turned down the hall and disappeared down the stairway. *Why a surprise tonight?*

Lily shuffled downstairs. Her stocking feet slipped out from under her toward the bottom. She landed hard on her rear and bounced down to the wood landing. The ridiculous situation set her off in a hysterical bout of giggles. And she'd thought the day couldn't get any worse.

Jack picked her up with Kelly looking on. "Are you all right, Lily?"

Lily almost snorted. "I'm fine. Sorry for the entrance."

A young, raven-haired beauty in a stylish red pencil skirt stepped forward. Her brown eyes skimmed over Lily. She offered a dainty hand forward. "Miss Lily, are you okay? I'm Jennie Lin. I hope this isn't a bad time."

Jennie cupped Lily's hand and gave it a reassuring pat. At least she knew how to put a clumsy teenager at ease.

"No, I'm good. Err—thanks though."

"Would you mind joining us so we can talk?" Jennie motioned to the couches as if she were the hostess.

"Sure." Jack and Kelly sat on the long couch and Jennie took the plush lounger. Lily plopped onto the love seat and hugged a pillow to her body. "Shoot."

Jennie held her hands prim and proper in her lap. "I'm here on behalf of Alturas Collective. Do you know about us?"

Was this girl serious?

"Uh, yeah? Just the company that launched the social network that has Facebook running scared, Twitter quaking in their boots, and Google smacking themselves in their foreheads. Who hasn't heard of Alturas and Flare?"

A little cough escaped Kelly's lips.

Lily noticed the shiny piece of tech on Jennie's wrist. "Ooh, is that the new Flare watch? Everyone at school is talking about it."

Jennie beamed and lifted her wrist to show off the shiny red device. "You're well-versed in your social media and technology. This is a prototype of a new model we hope to release later this year."

"Sweet. We lived near Seattle until last year, in the shadow of Microsoft. We just moved to Silicon Valley." She looked at her father with an apologetic shrug. "Sorry, Dad."

He cracked a rare smile. "Don't be."

Jennie tipped her head to the side, her brows furrowed.

"My dad works for a start-up tech company now. Microsoft is still a sore subject around here. Anyway, you're here with Alturas?"

The woman regained her composure, adjusting her band after tapping it a couple of times, her posture straight and true. "Yes.

Alturas has made great strides in the social media market. And we believe we have the answer for breaking through in a big way to make a huge difference in the world."

"Cool." Lily fingered the fringe on the pillow. Waited for more.

Jennie cleared her throat.

"Oh, sorry. I thought you were going to continue. So, what does that have to do with me?"

Jennie chuckled, the sound like a tinkling bell. "We've been looking for kids with great potential. Teens who can be examples to their peers."

Awareness dawned on Lily slowly. "And you think I'm one of those?"

Kelly raised an eyebrow as she glanced between Jennie and Lily. Dad's look was different, though. Pride. Delight. Something she hadn't seen in quite a while.

He leaned in. "What does this entail?"

Jennie cleared her throat. "In early June, we're having a special conference in Santa Clara at our campus. We're hosting the best and brightest from the West to bring them together and see what happens with their synergy and ambition. It'll be four days of intense interaction and collaboration. We want to see the strength of youth beamed out to every corner of the world."

Lily watched in amazement as her Dad's face transformed. He looked off into the distance, transfixed, and his wide smile grew. She'd overheard him discuss concerns about her with Kelly— though he'd never managed to ask Lily herself. Apparently, he was worried that Lily's potential was spiraling down. Did the idea of the conference resurrect old dreams he had for her?

Kelly brought the conversation back to reality. "You know, I'm Lily's stepmother, and I haven't been married to Jack for terribly long. Lily's a wonderful girl, but the recent years have been hard on her. Why was she chosen?" She looked at Lily with a soft grace in her brown eyes. "I think she's an incredible girl. I wonder, is this the best time for her?"

Jennie flashed her brightest smile. "We've been investigating potential youth for candidates throughout a wide region. Grades or concrete measurements aren't our main metric. We want potential to influence a generation. We've done a thorough investigation at her school, and despite her recent loss, we think Lily has something special to offer."

Lily raised her hand awkwardly. "That sounds pretty cool. I guess. But how are we going to pay for this? Dad, you're traveling all the time to make up the difference from the last year. My school is way expensive." Everett was something Lily could live without. Unfortunately, her leaving would break his heart. "And it's only three weeks away."

Another charming laugh from Jennie. "We know it's short notice, and we don't make this invitation lightly. It will all be covered. Simon is inviting you as a special guest, and he feels he would be a poor host if he didn't cover all your expenses."

A gulp caught in her throat and she almost choked. "I'm the guest of ... Simon Mazor?"

Kelly raised her hand. "Sorry, I'm the non-techie here, I guess. Who is Simon?"

Lily couldn't believe her stepmother. "Simon Mazor is the brains behind the Alturas Collective and the creator of Flare.

He's brilliant and a total hottie. He's like a combination of Mark Zuckerberg and Ryan Gosling."

"Ah. The Ryan Gosling part I get." Kelly blushed after her comment. Lily would normally tease her about that, but her mind stayed focused on a singular detail.

"So would I get to meet Simon?"

Jennie stretched her arms out wide. "You will, my dear. He's personally conducting the whole conference."

Dad still looked like he'd been hit with happy gas. Kelly must still be thinking about her Hollywood hunk. Lily rubbed her eyes. They must be tired or fried from that exploding stage light. Jennie had a weird dark sheen around her head, shimmering against her long, luxurious hair.

But never mind that. For once in too long, Lily recognized a sliver of hope, a spark that spread a small beam of light in her heart. Maybe life wasn't out to get her after all. Not if she could go meet Simon Mazor. She twirled her hair nervously. Glancing down, she saw no trace of black anymore.

Lily wondered if Simon liked blondes.

Chapter Seven

Somewhere in southeastern Europe

Shouts echoed through the dark, bouncing off the dank walls of the tunnel. Iaonnes didn't have much time.

Pale light from his phone screen illuminated the cobblestone path, but it didn't prevent Iaonnes from tripping. His weary knees crashed onto the damp stones, and a loud clank echoed from the object that caused his fall.

Did his pursuers hear that? Iaonnes had to keep moving. His curiosity held him back. He couldn't resist feeling for what tripped him. His hand brushed a piece of curved clay with winding cracks, probably from an ancient urn. How old was the treasure he just destroyed?

Probably not as old as he was.

His joints complained as he straightened up as best he could. The tight space of the underground tunnel slowed his progress. The Antiquities Ministry recently discovered these passages, hidden for millennia, and the opportunity to plumb a new archeological treasure from their rich soil excited the Greek officials, who had moved quickly to explore the ruins.

And by the commotion following him, they weren't pleased that he had snuck in. Iaonnes was happy to let them have it all once he obtained the information he needed.

Words he memorized long ago floated in his mind: *When these sacred paths are revealed, the time of worldwide darkness approaches. The gifts of heaven will be restored, and those anointed for such a time as this will find their call.*

Having fallen once already, Iaonnes took the descending stairs carefully. The discovery of the ruins signaled that the Archai had risen once more. After living in anonymity in the region for so long, quietly watching and waiting, it was finally time to fulfill his task of gathering and guiding those with talents needed for this situation.

He just needed to make it to the chamber before the authorities caught him. Then he would have his instructions for the next steps.

He'd lost many companions along the way, and now he journeyed alone. Iaonnes stayed content that the plan prepared for him adhered to the Father's will. His ways were not man's ways. He knew as an elder of God that those called would find the Enemy ready to oppose them. And the Enemy would tear the skies and the earth to corrupt and destroy the children of Light. His lips tightened at the thought of the Archai spreading their darkness again.

He pushed through a thick strand of silky webbing. These spiders' homes hadn't been disturbed in a long time. Soon archeologists would pore over every inch of this new discovery, teasing out faint secrets from the carvings and relics found here.

A wry smile spread across his face. If they knew what he could tell them, *he'd* be the relic they most desired.

Commotion carried through the serpentine tunnel. The men following him were getting closer. How much farther was it to the wall? He couldn't remember. Time jumbled together anymore. Iaonnes had kept many secrets and concealed many hiding places through the years.

The tunnel veered to the left, then straightened again. Iaonnes wanted to go faster, but the uneven ground forced him to keep one hand in front of him while the other held the phone toward the ground to guide his footing. His outstretched hand contacted a hard stone surface.

The tunnel ended with piles of thin stones stacked to the ceiling, blocking the passage. Slight gaps gave a tantalizing view beyond without yielding access.

Unless one was humble.

Iaonnes lay flat on his abdomen, his face against the stone floor. Dank odors overwhelmed his nose. He extended his arms above his head and made as much contact as he could with the cold surface. His fingers searched for the holes prepared long ago.

Angry voices bounced down the pathway. He'd soon have company, and they wouldn't be sympathetic to a trespasser. *"I'm sorry, but I had a divine mission to carry out. I'll be out shortly,"* probably wouldn't work.

He found the two holes and pushed his index fingers in. A thin stone lay within, and he pushed it down. A *clink* reverberated in the tunnel, and the renewed shouts from behind meant his pursuers had heard it.

It was time to enter.

Iaonnes let every muscle relax along his thin frame. He chanted a prayer in an ancient dialect, one of many languages he'd learned through the years. As he released himself to full faith, the slab sank beneath him. He marveled that something built specifically for his size and weight so long ago would work now.

As his slab lowered, more groaning came from the stones blocking the passage. Dust blew in the air as the stones turned on hidden posts from each side of the tunnel. Each stone turned clockwise, grinding against one another in a dull growl.

Panicked shouts sounded down the tunnel. Someone yelled in Greek, "Cave-in!"

The sound of their footsteps stopped. Hopefully worrying about a cave-in would buy the time needed for the aged mechanism to finish.

As the stones twisted apart and created an opening, Iaonnes's slab hit a track, and he slid forward through the opening. He held his breath to avoid inhaling the dust. Pebbles trickled over his back.

The movement stopped. Iaonnes rolled over and spasmed with coughs that spewed the dust away from his face. He stood with numerous pops in his joints, then stepped off the slab. The stones froze.

Although God gave him grace, he was getting too old for this.

The puzzle pieces of the barrier began to close again, slowly whirring as the pressure on the slab released. He moved, ready to find the chamber of light when a shout sounded behind him.

"You! Stop right there, by the authority of the Greek government!"

"My apologies, dear sir. I must answer to a higher authority." Iaonnes gave a slow bow as the shocked guard disappeared behind rock. He turned without another word and followed the tunnel, then ducked into a large hollowed-out cavern. He should have enough time with the timeworn mechanism keeping them at bay.

Etchings in the round cavern stretched from the entrance to a wood beam in the back and circled around to meet the other side of the door. Characters moved and danced on the walls, telling two stories.

The story on the right filled Iaonnes with memories of danger and miracles long ago. Fishing nets overflowing. A man walking on water. Soldiers coming for an innocent man. Pictures that spoke of the rise and fall of empires.

He could almost smell the sea spray and leather.

The left told of an adventure yet to come. His withered finger traced a figure near the beam. This one was in trouble. Another carving caught his eye. A brave soul would have to sacrifice. But out of the water the figure rose again. Baptism? A metaphor of resurrection, or something more?

Down toward the floor, one more figure seemed to bounce around the wall in a random pattern, breaking into the story. Could it be? That hadn't been seen in 2,000 years!

Yes, the time of gathering drew near. Iaonnes craned his neck to take in every detail. First, an initial coming together. Then trials. Some would stand, and some might fall. He knew God had a plan in store, yet the cost would be great.

Was this only the beginning?

He exhaled a long, worn-out sigh. After all this time, to see these marks again. Oh, to stay here and worship his Creator for His great wisdom and patience—but there was an appointed time ahead.

That, and the pounding of rocks crept into his subconscious. The authorities must be trying to break through.

Where was it? Iaonnes found a small wrapped package next to the beam. A beam that really wasn't needed for support. It stood for another purpose.

He took two stones out of a double-lined parchment wrap and bundled the inner wrap, dry and flaking, next to the base of the beam. It took several attempts of striking the stones until a spark caught in the parchment. A flame licked the beam, and it found a trail of resin that carried up the beam into the ceiling.

Iaonnes used the outer wrapping to cover his mouth from the acrid smoke filling the room. His faith was strong, even though doubt still flickered in the recesses of his mind. Would the contraption work after so long?

The top of the beam burst into a stronger fire, and a groaning sound accompanied a shaking of the whole chamber. He stepped into the door's threshold just as a circular piece of stone fell from the ceiling. A frayed rope ladder fell with the stone.

Iaonnes took one last glance at the antique carvings with a flash of regret. The fire would purge the symbols so no others could read the message. As the smoke billowed in the chamber, he gathered himself and ascended the ladder out of the darkened room.

It was time for his last journey.

PART
2

Chapter Eight

Streams of people milled about the circular fountain in the center of the walkway leading up to the Alturas Collective's headquarters. Demarcus turned around and around, pinching himself that he really had been invited to the Launch Conference.

I don't know how I ended up here, but thank you, Jesus.

Grassy knolls framed each side of the expansive walkway, with flowering hedges framing the outline of the campus entrance. Some sweet fragrance wafted through the air, giving the whole setting a magical atmosphere.

It was more than 3D. It was like a 4D experience. Without the dorky glasses.

He slung his backpack over his shoulder and sauntered to the edge of the fountain. Water cascaded off of multiple stars until it poured over a giant globe. The globe spun slowly on its axis, liquid trickling in its wake. The water sparkled fresh and clean in the sunshine. A perfect picture of all this day held.

Wait, he'd promised Mama lots of pictures, so this would be a good place to start. Demarcus pocketed his new Oakleys, a surprise gift from his mom for making the conference. He tried to do a selfie. How could he frame the magnificent fountain with his massive noggin?

A blonde girl strolled by with a man in a blue striped polo. She turned her head and caught his eye. Boy, a guy could swim in those baby blues.

"Hey, excuse me? Would you mind taking my picture with this fountain? I need to send a pic to my mom."

The man nudged her forward. "We've got time, Kitten. Help him out."

The look on the girl's face made it clear that she wasn't thrilled about her father's use of her nickname in public. She came up and put her hand out for his phone.

"Thanks. I'm Demarcus, by the way."

"You're welcome." He got a hint of a smile but no name. Interesting.

The girl pointed to a spot by the fountain. Demarcus found his mark and she took a couple of steps to size up the shot. "Okay, on three …"

She counted down and his brain blanked on how to pose. Act cool? Cheesy smile? Before he could decide, Blondie looked at the screen and finally cracked a full smile. "You were going for the smolder?"

"What?"

Before he could say anything, she strode to him and dropped the phone in his cupped hands. "There you go." She twirled on her sandals and walked away, her long hair bouncing in soft waves in her wake.

Her dad gave her a funny look as she joined him and started off. Demarcus called out, "Thanks, uh …"

"Lily."

"Thank you, Lily. See you around?"

Lily gave a quick shrug and turned away without breaking her stride. Then she disappeared into the crowd of kids and parents.

For a moment, Demarcus considered that this could be a very interesting weekend. But, honestly, girls ranked low on his list of excitement. He scanned the buildings ahead. The main building's large glass panels reflected the sunlight all around. The red letters of ALTURAS in their familiar swooping font stretched over the entryway with a man-sized torch extending from the wall behind it. Flames danced from the top of the torch, moving to an unseen rhythm.

He took a step backward to set up another picture and almost tripped over someone. He stumbled and caught himself with one hand, then he straightened and faced the dude. "Hey man, you gotta watch out. I didn't see you there."

The guy's eyes darted around as he retreated a step. He ran his hands through his spiked red hair, but the strands stood firm, frozen by gel.

"I'm so sorry. I didn't mean to." This kid looked absolutely freaked out.

"It's okay, man. I'm not gonna beat you up or anything. I just didn't see you behind me. It's cool, though."

Red opened his mouth to speak, then bit his lip instead.

Rough crowd today. "I'm Demarcus Bartlett. What's your name?" He stuck his hand out.

"Uh, Harry." He offered his hand in return.

Demarcus pointed toward the banner welcoming Launch attendees. "You here for the conference?"

"Yeah, I was invited by Alturas."

"Same here. I think we all were. Pretty crazy, huh?"

"Yeah, my mum joked about them getting me mixed up with someone else." He gave a small snort. "Thanks a lot, you know?"

Demarcus examined the kid closely. Thin, not athletic-looking. His smile filled a narrow face. "You said 'mum.' Are you British?"

"No. My mum married an American. I grew up in Montana. So I use a few British terms out of habit. Throws people off."

No glasses or scar on his forehead. Demarcus guessed he was more a Weasley than a Potter. "But no accent?"

"Nope. But my mum thought it would be cool to name me after the prince, what with my red hair. I still can't believe she did that to me."

The two of them looked around, the awkward silence of just meeting someone falling over them. Demarcus kicked a rock off the sidewalk onto the neatly manicured grass.

Harry shivered despite the California heat, and the motion seemed to frighten him to death. His body tensed and he looked over his shoulder to search his surroundings.

"Uh, so are you from Silicon Valley?" Demarcus asked.

"Not really. We just moved from Kalispell, Montana a few months ago. My dad got laid off in the timber industry, so he got a job here."

"That's too bad. Well, as a native of the Golden State, let me welcome you. I'm from southern California, so this area's new to me also. What do you say we go check in and find out what's next?" This dude was going to be eaten up here. But hanging out with Harry would mean Demarcus wouldn't be alone either, and maybe he could keep Harry from getting in trouble.

Harry let out a long breath. "That sounds … great. Thanks. Do you know where the bathrooms are?"

Okay. Maybe this wasn't the best idea. He hooked his arm around freaked-out Harry's shoulder. "I don't know, but let's start with a building. We just got indoor plumbing here last year."

Harry's eyes widened. "Really?"

Yeah, this could be a long weekend.

The janitor came out of the bathroom stall. Another porcelain pot shiny and ready for more mess. He walked out of the restroom in time to hold it open for an African-American kid escorting a red-haired boy.

The door closed behind the youth, and the janitor loaded his cleaning supplies and pushed his cart down the hall, his gaze sizing up the teenagers roaming the halls. Fifty youth here for this special meeting, and he was looking for at least three. When would they show themselves?

He adjusted his blue jumpsuit, straightening the fresh name patch on his chest. "John." He'd get used to it. He'd gotten used to many variations on his name over the years.

John arched his back and felt his old bones crack up and down. Time to get to work.

Chapter Nine

The show was about to start.

Simon Mazor leaned toward the curtain on the side of the stage. He could hear the murmuring and rumbling of the crowd in the amphitheater. All the excitement of the unknown. How sweet it was to tap into that energy and direct it. And if the Archai was right, the answer they sought sat in a seat out there right now.

His assistant Kelsey brushed stray lint off his jacket. He held his arms out so she could ensure he looked his best.

"All clear, Simon. You look fantastic."

Kelsey tilted her head and batted her eyes at him, a look he was used to by now. He shot her a sly wink, and she skittered off with an ecstatic grin plastered on her face.

He inhaled and exhaled a few deep breaths to center himself for the moment. This weekend marked a watershed opportunity for him. After all he had endured, throwing off the shackles imposed by his parents, now he stood at the cusp of offering freedom to an entire generation.

The work of Alturas and Flare was only the beginning. What would the world look like over the next twelve months? Simon wasn't sure, except that he knew the future would bear his imprint.

Simon stepped over to a side table to get his leather briefcase and typed in a code. A metal panel opened. He pressed his thumb against it. With a few clicks of the locking mechanism, the lid popped up. Two ebony cylinders embedded in a custom resin mold awaited him. He glanced around to ensure no one watched.

He took the black handles and warmth flooded his hands. The meter attached to the case began blinking red. His eyes squinted as he envisioned the following moments. Cheers. Excitement. People eating out of his hand.

The meter grew until reaching bright green bars at the other end.

In the corner near the curtain controls a router flashed. The signal from the Source reached it. That should set the stage.

He returned to the edge of the curtain, slipped a small resealable bag out of his jeans pocket, and pulled out a fresh gummy bear. Green. The most auspicious color. He smiled as he chewed the candy and let the sweet taste coat his mouth before swallowing.

Now he was ready.

Simon gave a thumbs-up to the technical director seated at the console on the other side of the stage, who nodded his head and flipped a switch to cut the lights. The sudden change hushed the audience.

Let the party begin.

Lily sat next to her dad in the center of the amphitheater. She scrunched down to minimize her profile. Most parents had just dropped their kids off at the campus. Only a few accompanied the other fifty kids to the opening ceremony. How'd she get so "lucky?" The Launch Conference was about empowering youth, and every other father had seemed to get the memo.

Not Jack Beausoliel.

She'd only had one interaction so far—the cute guy with dreadlocks by the fountain. And what a sweet gesture to send a picture to his mom. Hopefully the teens here were more like him and not like the Hot Tops. The last thing she needed was more drama.

The stage sat eerily quiet as people waited for the shindig to begin. A large flat-screen dominated the back of the stage, and large speakers hung from the upper scaffolding along with a rack of lighting. Some other large black boxes lined the sides of the stage with thick antennae sticking out toward the audience. Definitely fitting a hi-tech company.

When would they see Simon? That question dominated Lily's mind and probably everyone else's. The guy who broke the record for youngest billionaire had sent out a team to handpick everyone here. The thought of it blew her mind.

She twirled a strand of blonde hair around her finger. No black for the conference. It still fit her mood, but she didn't want any embarrassing style moments for the special weekend.

It still seemed strange how well Dad took to the idea. She hadn't exactly been the most cooperative child over the last year, with the remarriage to Kelly and her bucking his every attempt at moving on in life.

A feeling of shame washed over her. Yeah, life sucked. He didn't really deserve it, yet she had taken it out on him at every chance she could. They both were trying to climb out of the same muck caused by her mother's poor choices.

But here they were, together. Kelly had insisted that Dad be the one to take Lily, and Lily was thankful for that.

She took her father's hand and gave it a slight squeeze. He glanced down at her with a reassuring smile.

The lights illuminating the stage cut off, and the indistinct crowd noise hushed.

Wispy tendrils of white smoke filled the stage. Lily sniffed the air. Faint hints of vanilla and coconut wafted about the currents. Wow. A full-on sensory experience.

Low, haunting strains of a driving bass beat seemed to emanate from below their seats and lift into the air. The dubstep music started a throbbing pulse that built to an engulfing crescendo.

At the moment of musical climax, streaks of colored light intersected across the foggy canvas. Glittering and pulsing, the lasers flashed up and down in time with the music.

The intensity of the light shards pinwheeling around the stage enthralled Lily. She'd never considered how beautiful such piercing beams could be. The light show spoke something to her—she could feel a connection deep within herself.

This was crazy. How did this fancy get-up worm its way into her psyche? And yet her fingers yearned to draw with the same type of intensity. She lifted a single finger into the air.

Just focus, girl.

Her trance broke when the soundtrack dropped out and a confluence of beams, arrayed like a fan, separated. From the clearing mist emerged Simon Mazor.

He held his hands open in a simple gesture of welcome.

The crowd erupted.

Lily found herself on her feet, shouts of amazement coming from her lips. How cool was this?

The cheers took a full five minutes before they even started to settle. Simon took a few steps to each side of the stage, putting his hands together in a prayer motion and bowing to the adoring crowd. Eventually he signaled them to bring their decibels down to afterburner level.

Lily watched his eyes cross over her, and she swore his lips parted in a smile at the same moment. His V-neck T-shirt under a casual blue blazer epitomized the definition of Silicon Valley cool. He flipped a lock of black hair away from his eyes. That got a few extra cheers from a couple of lucky girls up front.

Lily had admired Simon at home, but she didn't know why she'd joined with the mass worship here. She glanced at Dad, who sat transfixed and subdued.

Simon gathered himself to speak, then stopped to leave everyone hanging a few more seconds. He gave his trademark grin and launched into his welcome.

"Thank you all for such an awesome greeting. And thank you for coming to the first ever Alturas-sponsored Launch Conference. Do you want to know the theme of our time together?"

More shrieks and applause resounded.

"'Free to be Free.' That's the message we want to get across here. You are the beginning. You have been chosen as a vanguard to go out there and turn the world around. There is so much amazing potential here in this theater. Your peers have much to offer. But you—" He pointed around the seats. "—have the keys to unlock a generation."

Another round of applause erupted. Lily wondered what had taken hold of the crowd, yet she joined with the chorus of cheers and clapped until her hands turned tingly. Just like the day when Clara was almost crushed under the spotlight.

Simon waved stop to the audience, and the place froze in silence.

"You see, we realized something here at Alturas. In coming together and working on Flare and seeing so many people brought together, we saw that we're living a lessened life. What is this? It's the lie that we're too small to make a difference.

"You might be sitting out there wondering, 'Why me?' Why were you chosen to come here? The thing is, alone you may not amount to much. Alone you won't make much difference in the world. You may question why you are even here?"

Lily shook her head. That was a weird thing to say. She looked at her dad. He sat, hypnotized, focused on Simon.

Simon raised his arms in a flourish. "Well, put that thought out of your head. The point is being together. The power of networking. If we join together and start something now—this weekend—do you know what will happen?"

The suspense was palpable.

Simon could have yelled the next words like a fiery Baptist preacher on Sunday morning. Instead, he brought it down to an intense whisper that still carried to everyone there. Lily could sense it.

"This weekend a revolution will start. And *you* will be the epicenter."

His words hung in the atmosphere. They reverberated through Lily's mind. A revolution. She had the power to make something happen in this community.

Amazing.

"Everyone, make sure you go to the tables with the first letter of your last name. You'll get your room assignments, welcome packets, and your exclusive Flare smart bands. We've got a variety of designs, so I think you'll find one you like. Especially since they're all free Wi-Fi hot spots."

A final roar sounded from the youth.

Simon dismissed the crowd. The teens filed out in astonished silence. He smiled, thanking the Master for his own gift to be a revolutionary. And in the excitement of the speech, he thought he'd glimpsed his own personal key to launch Flare to world-wide domination.

He had glimpsed a girl who shined.

Kelsey and his other support staff gathered around him on the empty stage. All the participants had left the amphitheater to find their dorm rooms. Those who remained constituted his inner circle.

"All right, gang. This is it. I want detailed reports. Let me know when you find a standout. We should have a few with unique abilities here. And find me the girl of light. She's here."

Chapter Ten

L ily flopped onto the bed in her dorm room, her legs dangling over the end. What a head-rush. Her dad had finally left after a few hugs, and she had the room to herself for the moment. Everyone had met with an advisor for orientation and received their room assignments. She didn't know who her roommate would be, but it didn't matter. Not at this conference.

Simon's eyes replayed in her mind. Man, that guy was hypnotic. She wasn't fooling herself—it was a stupid schoolgirl crush. But a man with brains and charisma, along with his dimpled chin …

A girl could dream, right?

Giggles sounded down the hallway, breaking Lily out of her daydream. She popped up to check the room out. She wasn't familiar with dorm rooms at colleges. She guessed they were nothing like those at Alturas.

Smooth hardwood floors reflected the sunlight streaming in from the windows. Two modern art pieces in shades of red and white hung above both beds. Chrome lamps topped both night stands. Even the curtains were stylish, white material with black swirls on them. Very art deco.

She'd shaken her head so much this afternoon that she thought whiplash would hit. Lily got a drink out of the bathroom sink, and the water trickled down her tongue, pure and airy. No chemical residue like most California water. She smoothed her tank top down so the heart on it lay straight. Her red shorts complimented the outfit, and she had to admit it felt good to try for cute again.

Okay, Kelly, you were right. All black would have been a bad choice here.

Her phone trilled with a new message. Lily skipped to the bed and snatched it up. Clara wanted to know how things were going. And how Simon looked.

Her thumbs flew over the keypad, her thoughts tumbling out before she could be coherent. *Yes, Simon is dreamy. The conference is way cool. No, I haven't checked the fire escapes yet.*

Lily snapped a photo of her special Flare smart band. Intricate red flowers popped out of the white background. Clara responded with a green jealousy emoji. The Wi-Fi on it was pretty sweet. There had been no lag since Lily had synced her phone.

The light beaming through the break of the curtains beckoned to her. Lily pulled them apart, taking in the western sky and the streaking colors of the setting sun. What a view! When was the last time she had truly enjoyed the beauty of a sunset?

Dust motes danced along the edge of each ray shining through. Lily sighed. To live carefree like that seemed beyond reach. Pain stabbed her heart as the memory of her mother leaving with Luke to run errands flashed before her.

The setting sun had been gorgeous on that night as well. But with twilight came the horrible news …

The door clicked. Lily wiped away a loose tear and pulled the curtains shut. Her roommate must be coming in. The bands had been programmed for their rooms, so no keys had been issued. Everything had been thought out for the attendees.

Except one detail.

Lily dropped her phone on the bed as her roommate entered. A crash of bags followed.

"I can't believe this," Missy spat as she stood in the doorway, frozen in shock.

Just like Lily.

Chapter Eleven

Missy pointed at the welcome packet on Lily's bed. "Check your room assignment. It's got to be a mistake."

Lily's heart sank. How could this weekend turn horrible so fast? Being stuck with her biggest enemy from school? Seriously?

"How do you think I got in?" Lily thrust her wrist out.

Missy tried to kick a bag past the door in heels. Athletic, she was not. She stumbled toward the first bed, and Lily just managed to stifle a laugh.

Missy huffed and threw her welcome portfolio on the bed. She flipped it open, sending a few pages scattering in the air. "Where's the number for the advisor?"

Nails pinched into Lily's palms as she tried to restrain her anger. How had it come to this with Missy? Lily remembered the first time they met. Missy's brother had accidentally splashed her on the first day at school, and Missy had bailed Lily out with an extra uniform for the day.

A promising friendship that had detonated four months ago.

Lily pulled the curtains open again. The sun had dipped below the horizon, the night sky pushing away the light.

Missy paced around her pile of luggage while talking to the advisor. "We can't stay together. We know each other, and this won't be good." She stopped and tapped her toe, the rapping on the wood echoing in the room. "What do you mean, you'll figure it out tomorrow?"

Missy punched the call off with a huff and threw the phone on the bed. Her eyes raked over Lily, and waves of disdain shot from Missy's pointed eyebrows and snarling lips.

"They said it's too late to make any change tonight. I'm stuck with you." The last words dripped with venom.

Lily couldn't believe this. She stomped over to the door. "I'll get out of your hair. Sorry to inconvenience you." Missy's snarling mouth was the last thing she saw as the door slammed shut.

Demarcus leaned against a pillar in the atrium of the Alturas dormitories. He flicked through updates on his phone and fired off messages to his buddies. He tapped out some smack-talk to his friend Nathan, who could never understand why Demarcus liked the Dallas Cowboys when they'd grown up in the backyard of the Chargers.

Demarcus's comeback never changed. He liked a winner.

He tapped his foot to hear the echoes in the vaulted room. This was nuts. Here he was on the latest and greatest tech campus in the country, ready to launch into … well, something. Everyone was sure excited by Simon's welcome a couple hours ago, but

Demarcus couldn't really remember anything of substance. He just knew he was excited to make a difference. Somehow.

The participants had filtered through the orientation tables after the opening presentation. Tomorrow they would meet for breakfast in the cafeteria and get assigned to small groups for their breakthrough sessions.

Now he killed time waiting for his roommate—Harry Wales. What a coincidence he'd ran right into him before everything had started. Harry was a nice guy even if he was terribly jumpy.

Right away Demarcus had sensed that the kid could use someone looking out for him. Harry's hometown was a small city near Glacier National Park, and he didn't seem to understand a big city or life outside of the woods. The two might make an odd couple, but it was cool to be a brother to someone and walk them through the culture shock. When Demarcus moved to the area, he didn't have someone to stand by him.

Yellow beams of sunlight dropped behind the horizon. Out east, twilight was growing and an early star was out. If Harry didn't hurry, they'd be wandering around in the dark. What was taking him so long?

A girl walked past him and pushed out of the glass doors. She stopped at the stairs and scanned the area before descending. Something about her struck him.

Was she from his school?

Demarcus checked to see if Harry had arrived. No redhead yet. Okay, he had to check this out.

He slipped out the doors and saw the girl's dark hair dance with her hurried steps. It'd be fun to dash in front of her, but he wasn't sure if she'd seen him in the atrium. He followed along slowly instead.

The girl rounded the corner of the boys' dorm, glancing around as she slunk toward the shadows developing. Her brown skin and the birthmark on her cheek sold it.

Rosa Gonzalez, a girl from his computer class who'd just graduated.

Okay, this was getting interesting. What he could remember about Rosa was her fiery attitude. He didn't know if she was the best student. So what kind of kid was Alturas after?

He paused at the corner, trying to decide whether to turn after her. Could he say hey and not miss Harry if came looking for him?

Rosa walked to the edge of the building, looking up at an open third floor window.

A voice called out, "Demarcus? You there?"

Demarcus turned to see Harry standing at the bottom of the stairs. He waved Harry over, intending to introduce him to Rosa.

She was gone.

.

Chapter Twelve

*W*hat?

Demarcus stepped forward, searching all around. No sign of her. The open window on the third floor clicked shut, but that was it.

Where had she disappeared to? Did he just miss her? No, there was no way Rosa could get by him. Unless she was fast too.

Was he the only gifted one at this conference, or was there more to the whole gathering?

He chuckled to himself. Yeah, he'd probably watched too many comic book movies. But the consideration still nagged at the edge of his thoughts.

Harry rounded the edge. "Dude, where are you? What are you doing?"

"Right here, Prince." He didn't want to sound crazy since they'd just met. "I'm looking for you."

Harry shuffled over with a raised eyebrow at Demarcus's lame excuse. "Heh, that's what my mum calls me."

They stepped out into the night air as a canopy of dark slowly settled over the grounds. Lights flickered on paths across the campus. "So your mom is British and married a lumberjack?"

"Yeah. Sounds like a Monty Python skit, doesn't it?"

Harry was fun to be with when he wasn't so jumpy. Still, the differences between them made him wonder all the more what had brought them together here.

A rumble through Demarcus's abdomen changed his focus, though.

"Dude, you need a California experience. Hungry?"

Harry felt his stomach. "I guess. Wasn't dinner enough?"

"What? They gave us wraps and milk boxes. Not nearly enough for us growing boys. I saw an In-N-Out Burger on the way here. I bet they didn't have those in Montana. Have you been to one yet?"

"I thought we were supposed to stay on campus. Will we get in trouble?"

Demarcus did a three-sixty to scan for chaperones or staff. All clear. "Man, we're not gonna cause trouble. We just need more grub, that's all. We'll get it to go and eat it here. No worries, man."

They strolled to the parking lot and cut across. Cars had to access through a manned gate, with a bypass for pedestrians. The burger joint was only a block away. It was probably a busy location being so close to a large workforce.

They hit the corner and Demarcus hit the button for the walk signal. He would've liked to dash across in a blink, but he hadn't told anyone about his gift yet. Harry seemed solid, but it wasn't time.

The stoplight turned and Demarcus tugged Harry's arm. They jogged past the cars waiting and hightailed it to the restaurant. The scent of freshly grilled beef floated by, and his saliva hit overdrive, triggered by the delicious smell.

They waited patiently in line, and he explained the choices to Harry, whose eyes lit up. He surprised Demarcus by ordering a triple-patty burger when their turn came. Demarcus had to get the Animal Style from the secret menu, and he insisted they get milkshakes as well. They nabbed their prizes and pushed through the doors.

The campus was quiet as they hit the parking lot. No need for stealth. Demarcus was ready to tear the bag open right there, when Harry stopped in the middle of the lot.

"Dude, c'mon. I'm really hungry. Let's get to the room," Demarcus said.

"There's someone watching. We're in trouble." Harry pointed to the side of the nearest building. A silhouette stood next to the stairs.

Demarcus couldn't tell if the person was watching them or not.

"Oh, no … it can't happen now!" Harry's face froze in a mask of panic.

"What's wrong? Don't worry, we'll explain ourselves."

Harry stood ramrod straight, his arms wrapped around his body like he was trying to keep himself together.

"Let's just get out of here." Demarcus looked back and the shadowy figure was gone. "See? It's fine."

He turned to find empty air.

Chapter Thirteen

Demarcus stared at nothing. Harry was gone. Disappeared.

"Harry? Where are you?"

A scream sounded from behind, and Demarcus whirled around. In the middle of the intersection they'd just crossed, Harry stood like a statue.

Smack in front of a car barreling toward him.

Demarcus dropped his bag of goodies and sprinted forward. The air whistled by as he rushed up to Harry and tackled him. The momentum carried them, skidding, to the edge of the sidewalk.

The car careened through the intersection with a loud honk, and then it was gone.

The two boys picked themselves up and retreated to a bus stop bench a few feet away. Demarcus rubbed a bad spot of road rash on his left arm. Gravel was embedded in his raw skin.

Something cold covered the front of his shorts, and he looked down. Pink ice cream dribbled down his leg. Harry held up an empty bag with the bottom ripped out. His dinner formed a trail leading from the middle of the road to where they sat.

Adrenaline fired through Demarcus's veins from the sudden burst of speed required to rescue Harry.

"What on earth were you doing in the middle of the road? Are you crazy? You could've been killed." Demarcus shook Harry to break the vacant staring-into-space look on his face.

Harry trembled on the bench. "I … I'm so sorry. So, so sorry. I shouldn't have come to the conference. I don't know what's going on. I thought they'd be able to help me."

Demarcus held his tongue. He wanted to keep yelling, but something was terrifying Harry. His pale skin looked sickly, and he shook with a fine tremor. Whatever had happened, Harry apparently couldn't control it and certainly hadn't planned it.

Demarcus put his arm around him to steady him. "It's all right, man. You're alive. I got you."

The pair sat in silence for a couple of minutes. Harry groaned and twisted his neck. Demarcus could see a clump of blood on the back of his head, camouflaged by his red hair. He wadded up the broken bag and dabbed at the wound.

"Are you hurt anywhere else?"

Harry turned his hands around to examine them. One side had scraped knuckles.

"I think it's mostly my head and my butt. We landed pretty hard." Harry turned to face him. "How about you?"

Demarcus held up his left arm. The limb complained with the motion—it would be fun to use tomorrow. Harry gasped at the sight. Not a good sign.

"Let's get back over to the campus," Demarcus said. "I left my food behind. We can split it. But what just happened?"

The duo limped across the walkway. Harry lowered his head and shrugged. "Just a mistake."

No, that answer wouldn't do. Something was up. Demarcus held a hand out, blocking Harry's path. "C'mon, man. I just saved your life. I think I deserve an explanation."

Harry squinted and bared his teeth. "I don't know what's going on. Sometimes I just … I just end up somewhere else."

Demarcus couldn't hold back a small laugh. "Yeah, right. You just teleport into harm's way?"

Harry raised his head and caught Demarcus's gaze. His eyes glistened in the light of the streetlamp. "Not always into danger. But yeah, I just disappear and end up somewhere else. I can kinda feel it coming on, and I try to stop it. Sometimes it seems to work. Other times—well, you saw what happened."

Demarcus shook his head, questions pinging in his skull. "What do you mean? That's like a comic book stunt."

"I'm pretty sure I'm nothing like a comic book."

"Isn't there anything you can do? Can you direct it?"

"I can't figure out how to control where I'm going. I've been in some strange circumstances so far. Up a tree. In the middle of a stream." Harry's eyes flared. "I just want to get rid of it. I'm hoping maybe something or someone here can help me."

Demarcus loved his ability so much. What would it be like to have one seem like a curse instead of a blessing?

They stepped over the curb and it was Harry's turn to bring up a question. "So how did you get to me so fast? I was a good sixty, seventy yards away."

Uh-oh. What could he say to keep from revealing his speed?

"I think it was the adrenaline rush, dude. I saw you in trouble, and I just hustled out there."

Realization dawned on his face as Harry wagged his finger at him. "No way. I looked up and saw you flat-footed in shock, and the next thing I know you're in my face and we're skidding on the asphalt. Fess up. You've got a secret too."

Demarcus kicked a rock on the ground, bouncing it under a car. He didn't know what Harry would do with his secret, but what was he going to do now?

"Yeah. I broke my ankle this spring and had to be in a walking boot. When I got out of it, I went to a field to test out the strength with some running. I started going faster and faster. Now I outrace cars on the highway. Just now I think I had a bigger burst coming after you."

Harry's eyes widened to the size of saucers. "Whoa. So you're like the Flash?"

He couldn't help a chuckle. "Naw. I don't think I could run on water or go supersonic. But how cool is this? We've got super powers!"

They reached the spot where Demarcus left his meal. They found nothing on the ground. "Oh, no. Where's my grub?"

A white-haired man stepped from behind a truck. In his hand he held the white bag with the goodies from In-N-Out. He extended it toward them.

"You don't have super powers," he said. "You have gifts. The question is, what will you do with them?"

Chapter Fourteen

Demarcus and Harry shared a look as the stranger led them to a side building and into a vacant meeting room. A street lamp shining through the window provided the only illumination.

Demarcus didn't want to draw attention to the conversation about to happen, especially since they'd already spilled the beans in front of the fossil who'd brought them here. He hoped that this out-of-the-way area the old man picked would do the trick, far from the dorms and the main conference buildings.

The three of them sat at the elongated conference table in an awkward silence. Harry held his head in his hands. Demarcus didn't know what to do, but he snuck a fry out of the bag and popped it in his mouth. His sprint had made him even hungrier.

The silvery glow from outside framed their guide. His head looked like it had a halo, light reflecting off the remaining whitish wisps of hair that stubbornly held on to his scalp.

Despite the weird circumstances, peace radiated from the man. And he didn't act surprised about the boys' conversation.

Instead of being incredulous about their claims, he'd corrected what they said.

The elderly dude gave them a warm, grandfatherly smile. "I'm sorry to have spooked you boys out there. You can call me John."

Demarcus suddenly noticed a lanyard with a picture badge around the guy's neck. He wondered where he was from. His skin had a darker hue and his accent sounded, well, he couldn't quite place it. Middle Eastern? Maybe Spanish or even Greek?

"Uh, so I'm Demarcus. This here is my new friend Harry."

Harry looked up with a start. "Are we in trouble? I knew we shouldn't have gone off campus."

John chuckled, a bass sound rumbling from his chest. "Foraging for food? No, you are quite all right there, young Harry. In fact, please partake of your food before it gets too cold. I understand these sandwiches are best enjoyed warm."

Okay. The dude was definitely an immigrant. Demarcus wasn't going to argue with the permission to eat, so he pulled the burger into rough halves and slid one over to his roomie. A loose pickle plopped onto the table, and in a blink, he nabbed it and popped it into his mouth.

"So you said something about super powers. Yeah. That was something we were goofing on. What kind of power we'd like to have if we could." Demarcus followed with a nervous laugh. Was John senile enough to buy it?

John folded his arms across his chest, his bushy eyebrows furrowed. "I have seen many things in my time. I know when I've seen something amazing, so don't try to fool me, son. My body may be tired, but my mind knows what it saw."

Demarcus shivered with the realization that he had been caught.

"I saw destiny. I saw gifts being used. I saw the Lord's anointed. Thankfully, I saw what I have been waiting to see for a long time. There are a few of you here that I have been looking for."

Demarcus set his milkshake down, his appetite suddenly diminished. "Um, that's cool. What does that all mean?"

"It means we have a lot to talk about."

Harry ran a hand through his hair. "Mr., uh, John? How can this be destiny? I almost got killed out there because of this crazy thing that happens to me. I didn't ask for it. I don't want it."

"Boys, let me tell you a story. There was a man born in a time of great need. His people lived in peril. They needed a deliverer. His parents made a promise that their son would be held to a special vow before God.

"This boy grew up with great strength, and he soon defended his people against the evil ones who tried to rule them. He became a man, but a man who was proud and foolish, thinking he was unstoppable. In a moment of weakness, he revealed his one vulnerability: his hair."

Demarcus stopped chewing. "Samson?"

John pointed a bony finger at him. "Exactly right. He gave his secret to the temptress Delilah. His hair was shorn, and he lost his power. His enemies captured him, put out his eyes, and paraded him in their temple during a festival. His hair had started to grow back, and in a final moment of humility, he cried out to the Lord for his strength to be returned. His prayer was answered, and he knocked the pillars of the temple down, dealing a terrible blow to the enemies of Israel, at the cost of his own life."

Harry looked confused. "I've heard the Bible story before. What does that have to do with us? I wish I had strength instead of whatever it is I have."

John's wizened hand rested on Harry's shoulder. "The story means, my young friend, that the Lord gives gifts to His people as He sees fit. Samson was not the best example for Israel. He was prideful, haughty, and a fool. He was not chosen because of who he was. All of God's children are given gifts. It is up to them to determine how they will be used. Will we use them to serve the Lord, or serve ourselves? If we think only of ourselves, we ultimately serve the Enemy."

Demarcus leaned in, the implications of the conversation hitting him like waves of surf. "Wait. You mean I can run fast and Harry can teleport or whatever he does for a reason that only God knows?"

"Yes! In your case, you have been given extraordinary gifts for a special time."

Demarcus tried to swallow. No saliva worked its way down his parched throat. "Okay. This is freaky."

Now John raised a finger to his mouth, paused, and then cleared his throat. "I am still figuring out the nuance of your tongue. I do not understand 'freaky.'"

"Well, I go to church. I believe in Jesus and all that, and I thought that God had given me this gift, because where else would it come from? But to be like a Samson? Does that make us some kind of deliverers?"

"Precisely."

Harry groaned. "I'm only fifteen. I don't shave yet. I can't drive a car. And I sometimes blip up into a tree or across the street in the middle of traffic. Yeah, I'll be a lot of help."

"Don't worry, young man. This can be a very confusing time. Why else were you brought here, but because of your gift?"

Harry stood up. "I'm sorry. I don't think I want to be a part of this. Demarcus, I'll see you at the room." Before John could react, Harry ducked out of the room. The outside door slammed shut.

Demarcus could've caught Harry, but the guy needed time to sort things out. And Demarcus had just taken another bite of his hamburger. His own mind buzzed with the revelations. Harry could … teleport? Their abilities were ordained?

"Oh, dear. I do need to work on my communication with the youth. What is the gap I've heard about?"

Demarcus scratched his chin. "You mean the generation gap?"

"That's the one. Well, at least you are still here. What do you think of this? I suppose it is a lot to share with someone all at once."

"Sir, my mother almost died when I was born. I never knew my father. We haven't ever owned a ton, but my mom always believed in two things: that God saved her and that God created me for a reason. Now Biblical heroes are big shoes to fill. Er, sandals … whatever. Anyway, you seem to know something, so I'm ready to listen."

John started to respond when Demarcus recalled Rosa's disappearing act earlier.

"Sorry, but you said you were looking for others like us? Are there more than Harry and me?"

John's grey head nodded. "There is a growing darkness, and your gifts were foretold long ago. I believe there's more than you and your confused friend. That is why I am here."

"Wait. You don't usually work here?"

John nodded. "I would have liked to retire a long time ago rather than pushing a broom around here. This conference is not by accident. Others are looking for you too."

Demarcus shook his head. This was getting way too deep. "What do you mean?"

"It is no coincidence that the Alturas Collective came around with this conference for special children, paying your way, right when you started running fast. I do not know the ultimate agenda here, if Alturas is the source, or if they're just a tool. Just know that other people are looking for you as well."

Demarcus pondered a shadowy conspiracy as he slurped the last of his vanilla shake.

"We have just met, and I know it is a lot to take in, yet I must ask for your help. I need assistance in discovering what is going on at the conference. Will you take an old man on faith and help?"

"Um, I guess I'll do what I can."

John beamed, his teeth crooked but otherwise looking good for an old guy. "This is wonderful news. I will meet with you after lunch tomorrow on the next step. Until then, please keep this between us."

No problem there, dude. If Demarcus told the staff about this, they'd think he was crazy.

The sound of a door closing made both of their heads jerk toward the hallway. "It seems the security is making their rounds," John whispered.

Demarcus's heart spooked like that of a stray cat. "What are we going to do? The light's on—they'll know someone's in here."

John reached over and snatched the fries and shake out of Demarcus's hands. "I am sorry to do this. I will replace your meal as soon as I can." He spread the food out as if someone had been eating there, and even dumped a glob of ice cream on the table. "Duck under the table. I will distract the security guard. Use your speed to get out of the building. I have an excuse to be here."

Demarcus started to protest, when the sound of approaching footsteps silenced his argument. He slipped under the table right before the door opened. The chairs along the table made it a tight fit. He tried to slide over toward the end closest to his escape route.

"What's going on in here?" a gruff voice asked.

All Demarcus could see was the dude's huge legs.

John let out a breath of air, mimicking disgust. "I was making my last check and I find this mess. Can you believe it?"

"I'll need to see your badge."

The guard stepped over toward John. This was his chance. Time to bolt.

Demarcus flashed into the hallway. No one else appeared to be there, and nothing sounded suspicious with John and the guard.

Way to push your luck. Don't get kicked out the first night. With that thought, Demarcus tiptoed to the front doors, hoping to avoid any more security on the way.

Chapter Fifteen

Lily wandered the halls until she found a quiet nook and broke the news to Clara about her new roommate. At least Clara's indomitable spirit had lifted Lily out of the blues, suggesting several pranks to pull on Missy, each more ridiculous than the last. Lily's favorite was shaving one eyebrow. Not that she—or Clara—would actually do any of them.

Still, she'd been so excited for the conference, only to have her biggest rival as her roommate? It had to be a cruel trick.

When she returned to the room, the chill in the air could've frozen lava. The two danced around each other as they got ready for bed. This morning, Lily made sure to get up early. Missy had barely stirred by the time she tiptoed out of the room.

Now Lily stood motionless in the doorway of the cafeteria like it was the first day of high school. Who were the cool kids? What cliques were forming? Memories of prior experiences in Washington and again at Everett Academy bubbled inside her gut, a stew of anxiety and fear. Ugh. And Missy would be waiting for her back at the room. Was the conference worth it?

She thought of Clara's encouragement the night before. Here she was, chosen for a special gathering, yet paralyzed by the thought of sitting at a table—the dark side of adolescence. She could do this. She would do this.

A woman brushed by her, and Lily instinctively flinched. However, a familiar face turned. Jennie Lin escorted another girl through the doorway.

"Lily, so good to see you. How are you doing today?"

"Uh, I'm fine. I guess," Lily said.

"Would you like to join us? I need to talk to you about your roommate situation." Jennie pointed to the girl at her side. The girl shyly lifted a hand in a meek wave. "Sarah, this is Lily."

"I actually go by Sarah Jane, if you would."

Lily offered a wave of her own. Sarah Jane pushed a strand of strawberry blond hair behind her ear. A smattering of large freckles covered the girl's round face, and her pink complexion flushed brighter.

"Sure, I'll join you," Lily said, wondering when she'd be able to ask Jennie about Missy.

The girls joined one of the food lines. An efficient buffet served all sorts of fruit, muffins, and hot breakfast foods. Lily picked out an egg-white omelet with spinach and mushrooms. Her Seattle roots required a trip to the espresso bar, so she joined her companions a few minutes after her steaming cup of dark liquid energy was ready to go.

Jennie wasted no time. "I'm very sorry about the situation with your current roommate. I understand the girl you were paired with is not a good match."

Understatement of the year. "Yeah, we go to school together. She's kinda my nemesis. Last night was not cool."

"I understand. She was on the phone to her advisor, uh, rather forcefully last night. We have made arrangements to trade rooms. We're going to have you move in with Sarah here."

Lily and Sarah Jane regarded one another. She seemed nice enough, and anything would be better than Missy Austin.

Their attention shifted as monitors flickered on across the meal hall. Simon flashed onto the screens with a plaid button-down shirt and a large smile.

"How is everyone this morning? Are you ready for a world-changing day? I hope you got some good rest, because we're off and running now. Report to your group labs after breakfast, and I'll talk to you at lunch. Here's to your potential!"

The sight of Simon's handsome face on the TV feed lifted Lily's spirits immensely. It might be stupid, but she pictured him speaking directly to her.

Jennie took a drink of her green tea. Strange. A faint, dark aura glowed around her head again, just like at their first visit at her house. Lily needed to ask what conditioner she used, to get such an effect.

Jennie noticed Lily's stare. "Is everything all right? You seem distracted."

"Oh, I just need my eyes checked when I get home is all." She turned to Sarah Jane. "Where are you from?"

She spoke with a quiet, high-pitched voice. "I'm originally from Phoenix. Terrible place for someone with my complexion. We just moved to Fremont in January."

At least she had enough self-confidence to kid about herself. Lily didn't know if she could do that right now. She took a swig of her cappuccino. Why couldn't her magic coffee elixir grant her that kind of moxie?

Jennie clapped her hands. "I'm so excited for you girls to experience all that we're offering this weekend. I've grown so much working for Alturas, and the opportunity to spend the next few days drawing out your gifts will be invaluable."

Lily twisted the ring on her right hand, a silver band topped with a black onyx. A present from Kelly to commemorate the big trip. Kelly was still trying to reach out, and this little gesture had actually made a difference. She seemed to realize Lily had some darkness to deal with, and she didn't fight against it. The onyx was a good touch.

"Will we learn how we were selected? I've been going over your visit since then, and I still don't get the potential and influence bit," Lily said.

Sarah Jane nodded. "Really. I'm the last person I would've picked from my school. This is cool, don't get me wrong. It just doesn't make sense."

Jennie's eyes widened, and she picked at her Flare band while seemingly searching for a response. Weird. Normally she came across as so confident. "Everyone is different. That's what makes this conference unique—that the attendees are all unique. Lily, we saw something in you that will be different for Sarah."

Lily noticed a mild scowl from Sarah Jane at the continued whiff of her name. She waved her hand at the other kids. "So that's it? There's a generic uniqueness that we all happen to share."

Jennie didn't let herself get ruffled any further. "All I can say is that you'll be amazed. We need to hurry up though, or you'll be late for your group labs."

Lily followed through with a last bite of her omelet while Sarah Jane munched on an apple. The girls stood up and deposited their plates at the trash, except for Lily's coffee. Nope, she would drain that cup of everything it contained.

Jennie checked her phone. "You girls have a change in your group lab. You will report to lab 11-M, upstairs in the Golden Hall. Do you remember where that is from orientation?"

"We're both changing groups?" Lily asked.

"Yes. We had some last-minute inspiration, and there was a little shuffling. You'll find being at Alturas requires some flexibility. Off you go."

Lily shrugged at the change. Since she didn't have any expectations, shifting around didn't bother her. At least her awful roommate had been changed. Now she could avoid Missy and enjoy the opportunity.

She followed Sarah Jane out the door, and they headed for their assigned lab.

Simon waited at the conference hall across from the cafeteria. The teens had filtered out of the building and headed toward their labs. He remained confident that their screening process had picked up kids with influence and malleability, each with the ability to go back home and be Alturas's ambassadors on a local scale. Now, if their further winnowing could pick out the few who were truly special, their plans could advance so much faster.

He popped a yellow gummy bear into his mouth. Not as confident as green, but a good sign nonetheless. Simon continued watching recordings from security of the attendees spilling out of the cafeteria toward their appointments. He smiled as the level of excitement amongst the teens remained buoyant. No signs of anyone special so far this morning.

A few of his staff trickled in, having gone through to find particular individuals at breakfast and redirect them to their special labs. Jennie Lin and four others took their seats around the table. They discussed things for a few minutes, then their group went silent.

Simon turned from the monitors to address them. "So, were you discreet? And did you get everyone?"

Jennie stood up to report for the group. "Yes, sir. We intercepted all of the girls who had light colored hair. They'll be in 11-M."

Simon couldn't identify the girl who'd glowed out of the crowd. All he could tell from the stage was a golden aura around her hair. It couldn't be any with dark hair, so with a little targeted adjustment they'd whittled down the investigation group. The next test should narrow things down further. Who would be the one with the gift his project desperately needed?

Chapter Sixteen

"Come on. You're going so slow."

Harry jogged to the stairs. "Hey, I'm not the one with super speed."

Demarcus did a facepalm. Did the kid really say that out loud?

After talking with John for a while, he'd left the mysterious custodian and found Harry asleep in their room. No chance to talk about the revelations from the evening and why Harry had left.

Then he hadn't heard the alarm on his phone. Harry had forgotten to set his, and they'd managed to sleep through all of the others in their hall leaving for breakfast. If it weren't for Harry falling out of his bed, they still wouldn't be awake yet.

They scurried down the stairs and out the doors. Demarcus had to consciously hold back, for Harry's sake. His arm appreciated avoiding any jarring, as it still throbbed some from last night.

"So why did you fall out of bed?"

Harry rubbed his head. "I was dreaming about teleporting into the intersection again. You know how you'll jerk if you dream you're falling? I think it was like that. And I landed right on my goose egg from last night."

"Dude, have you ever read any comic books?"

"Yeah."

"Isn't the first rule something about not talking about your powers in public?"

Harry shook his head. "I think it's more, 'with great power comes great responsibility.' Either that or 'no capes.'"

Demarcus pushed the door open for the cafeteria building. His stomach dropped when he heard nothing but the echo of the door hitting the side of the entryway. Had they missed breakfast?

They ducked into the meal hall. The kitchen staff was finishing up polishing the silver buffet tables and sweeping the floors.

A worker looked up at them with an eyebrow raised. "Did you guys forget something?"

"Yeah, our alarms. Is there any breakfast left?" Demarcus asked.

The woman wiped her hands on her white apron while a corner of her mouth pulled up in annoyance. "I'm afraid not. I can pull some fruit out, but that's it. You really are late."

No bacon? Shoot. Demarcus could smell the lingering scent of sizzling pig. This was going to mess with his whole day.

Harry's shoulders slumped. "You mean I don't have time for a cup of tea?"

Demarcus turned to him. "Really, dude?"

The cook pulled out a bowl of fruit and slammed it on the counter.

The boys both grabbed bananas and apples. Hopefully they could eat in their group lab. They hollered their thanks as they hit the door. Demarcus started to accelerate too quickly to make up time. With a crunch, he smacked into the back of someone. Both bodies tumbled into a heap on the floor.

He scrambled off the guy. "I am so sorry—"

Demarcus had just run over Simon Mazor.

"Oh, wow. I am really sorry. Here, let me help you up."

Simon took Demarcus's extended hand, Demarcus pulled the billionaire entrepreneur up. What a stupid mistake.

"Don't worry. I'm okay. What are you guys doing?" Simon straightened his shirt as an assistant rushed over to check on him.

"Uh, we just overslept and snagged some fruit before going to lab."

Simon looked down the hall with a curious look on his face. "You just left the cafeteria?"

Demarcus looked at Harry, who stood as still as a statue. "Yes, sir."

"The cafeteria that is ten yards away?"

He hadn't noticed the distance. He'd just barely cleared the doors. At least, that's what he thought. Sure enough, the doors were down the hall.

Simon scratched his head. "Please be more careful. Not paying attention for that long, we don't want any conference attendees to get hurt." He looked at his watch. "You'd better get moving, guys. You're late for lab. You don't want to miss that. I can't wait to see what you all come up with." A wide smile spread over his lips.

Harry tugged on Demarcus's arm. Yeah, time to go. After the initial shock of hitting Simon, he wanted to hang with their host. But Simon had said go.

"Again, so sorry, sir. Thank you, Mr. Mazor. See you later."

"He gets the picture. Excuse us, please." Harry finally pulled Demarcus out of his star-struck daze to get moving. They pushed out the doors, looking for Redwoods Hall.

"Wow. I just met Simon," Demarcus said.

Harry raised an eyebrow. "Yep, made quite an impression. Literally. I think he'll have a mark on his chest now."

"Did I really go fast?"

Harry shrugged. "You turned the corner pretty fast, so I didn't see what happened. Maybe."

"Great."

Simon rubbed his lower back where the kid ran into him. The teen was a little shorter than him, but he packed a wallop. He was about to go on with his next appointment when a thought hit him.

"Kelsey?"

The brunette jumped to his side. "What do you need, Simon?"

"It's 8:35 A.M. Go to security and have them check the footage of my little encounter here. I might have just run into our next exceptional candidate."

Chapter Seventeen

L ily sat in a world of blonde.

Seriously. This was supposed to be an epic conference with special youth, and they gather all the blondes together in one room? How original is that? At least that left Missy out for now.

Sarah Jane sat next to her, along with seven other girls. The glass room let in all of the morning light, and the smooth white furnishings added to the gleam. She wondered if they'd hand out sunglasses to protect their eyes.

The two female leaders came in from the door on the left. The women wore knee-length lab coats and matching light blue polos and khaki pants. The pair screamed conformity. They looked around the room and gave the big Alturas smile.

"Welcome, everyone. I'm Alexia, and this is Belinda. We're excited to have you for our first lab of the weekend. I can say that I think your minds will be blown here, so we won't waste time."

Lily raised her hand and simultaneously blurted out, "What's the purpose of this session?"

Alexia pointed at her after the fact. "You had a question. Well, your groups will rotate to different stations as the weekend progresses, so make friends along the way. You'll be mixing and matching in various combinations." She glanced at her partner. "I can tell you that I think this one is the coolest we've got going. But like I said, why wait? Everyone come up here."

Lily rolled her eyes and heaved herself out of the chair. The two techs led them to the front of the room where a large pillar embedded in the wall formed a half cylinder. Belinda slid open a panel and tapped in a code.

A whirring started and the room shuddered a little. As Lily glanced around to see if it was an earthquake, the rest of the group let out a collective, "Ooooh."

She turned back and saw what the big deal was. "Oooh."

The smooth wall of the pillar retracted, revealing a large hole in the floor. A fireman's pole threaded through the middle.

Belinda flipped her coattails behind her, grabbed the pole, and slid down through the gap. Alexia turned, her orange curls flipping behind her. "Who's next?"

A petite girl standing in the front recoiled a little. "You want us to go down that?"

Alexia smiled wide. "Yep! Don't dawdle, everyone. Get down."

Sarah Jane and Lily shared a look. Why not? Lily stepped forward and reached for the pole. Now this was kinda cool. A sense of fun bubbled out of the two leaders, so why not play along? She hopped over the space and dropped down with a whizzing sound.

Stepping back to allow the others to come, she surveyed the room. If the last room was a glass house, this was the whitewashed room. Smooth rectangular panels of some kind of stone material formed the walls. The only structures in the room were ten hooks spaced evenly, five to a side. The hooks each held a spherical metallic frame, with the front angling into a point that had a blue lens on it.

She fingered the device. It looked like a helmet of some kind.

Her curiosity welled up. What were these guys up to?

One by one, there came a whoosh and a thud from girls sliding down the pole. The last girl was the fraidy-cat, who landed with a squeal. Alexia plopped down beside her and pulled out a small tablet computer from a lab pocket.

"Everyone gather along the sides and grab a Focuser."

The girls did what they were told. They each turned their weird appliances around, inspecting them. Alexia tapped a few times on her device and the pole retracted into the ceiling. The hooks did the same into the walls.

After everything retracted, the room resembled a plain white box. Packed with blondes. There didn't even seem to be a door. The washed-out walls and floors reflected light from glowing ceiling panels. Nothing stuck out from the walls at all. Perfectly symmetrical and sheer.

Okay, this was weird.

Their guides stepped into the center of the room. "Sorry, but it's more fun to experience it rather than being told. This is the room where each new group of interns and employees come to get started at Alturas. It's more than that, though. Everyone needs to put on her Focuser. It will fit like a helmet, with the blue piece in front."

Belinda demonstrated with the extra headset while Alexia did all the talking.

Sarah Jane poked at the inside of the space hat. Lily examined the circuitry around the lens. A very intricate pattern was engraved into the raised border. The metal band that held it was the purest silver color she had ever seen.

Well, this was part of the deal. Lily slipped the funky headgear on. Too bad there was no mirror. All the other girls looked like some kind of android. Her stomach fluttered with uncertainty.

Alexia paced the center of the room while Belinda stood where the pole had been. Alexia continued, "All right, ladies. This is our Focuser. It amplifies your core thoughts, the essence of who you are. We all have latent abilities, strengths, and talents. For most people it takes years to figure this out through trial and error.

"However, here at Alturas, we have worked hard to find keys to unlocking that centering principle of our lives, of our being. When you discover what you love—what resonates most with you—then you can chase that with passion and a drive that is unparalleled to just casting about, trying to find yourselves."

Belinda took two steps forward. The woman hadn't spoken yet, and when she talked, a lilting Aussie accent came forth. "You don't realize the privilege you're about to experience. This is going to shape your life. Are you ready?"

Lily glanced around, as did the rest of the girls in the group. *Well, we've already got the funky hats on. Why not?* She couldn't really imagine what the future held for her. A murky veil had draped over any hopes she'd once dream about for the future.

Alexia continued. "There aren't any objects in the room, no protrusions, because the Focuser needs to reflect off of the special surface here. It'll take about ten minutes, but it might feel like years pass by. When it activates, you'll hear a gentle sound, and your vision will wash out. You won't see anyone else. The sensory centers in your brain will override things, and you'll experience who you were meant to be."

Lily wanted to quip about a fancy 3D experience. The better plan was probably to hold her tongue.

"If you're ready, give me a thumbs-up sign."

Lily stuck out her thumb, ready to hitchhike in this strange circumstance.

"Belinda, power up."

The last thing Lily saw was the wide grin on Alexia's face.

Chapter Eighteen

A soft thrumming sounded behind Lily's ears. The helmet clamped down on her temples and the back of her head. The tightening startled her. What was this thing doing?

Her body froze. She couldn't move her arms. Her legs stiffened like oaks, rooted to the ground. If she'd wanted to tear the Focuser off, there was no way.

The scene before her faded into a whitewashed glow. A warm sensation flowed through her skin like waves. Heat massaged her body, filtering every cell from the outside in. Her bones radiated heat inside. She'd never experienced anything so comforting and relaxing. The anxiety from her immobility sank into the ground.

The soft radiance streaked past her eyes, and she plunged into darkness, inky and tangible. She floated now, and instead of her peasant blouse and shorts, she wore a flowing, thin linen gown that drifted around her body, her bare toes searching for footing. The fluid space around her chilled her skin wherever it touched. The warmth from a moment ago seeped from every pore, and she shivered from the change of temperature.

Lily tried swimming through the thickness, but she couldn't move through the murky substance. Claustrophobia tightened its tendrils around her body, encompassing her mind and her heart.

The dread overwhelmed her resolve not to panic. She wanted to thrash about, break through this muck, and find her core. *What kind of finding-yourself exercise was this?*

Now the lightless material forced her eyelids closed. It entered her ears, crawled up her nostrils, and dripped down her throat. Lily tried to clamp her mouth shut. The gloomy ooze seeped through her lips and past her clenched teeth. Her lungs seized. She was drowning in darkness.

She'd wanted to embrace the black over the last few months. Now it was taking her.

Her thoughts fuzzed, and she could barely hold on. *Please, I need help. Can't someone see I'm dying?*

Mercy!

The darksome material flinched. The progression of death stopped.

I need a way out!

The throes of midnight loosened its grip on her. She coughed and sputtered as it retreated from inside. Her eyes snapped open.

She could barely make out something in the distance. A light. A pinprick of something, the barest glimmer that seemed so far away. The tentacles of ice that held her fast didn't let go, but now there was something besides an absence of all hope. In her mind she focused on that light, willing it to brighten.

The single point twinkled.

What was that? It responded to her. There was something in this void that she could control.

It slipped back, fading from sight.

No! Lily needed that light.

Something in her chest clawed at the inside of her rib cage. She strained forward, wriggling her hand to move, just a fraction at first. Her fingers flexed and curled. If she could point at the light before it winked out …

Her index finger straightened and she concentrated on forming a line from her fingertip to the tiny spark out there. *Come on.*

No more darkness!

A blaze erupted.

The thick gel that enveloped her burned away. The faraway star that rescued her wasn't the only light anymore. Sparkles popped up all around, dotting the black canvas. Lily laughed as she spun around in a floating pirouette. The new glints of starlight danced with her.

Her hands! She held them up in front of her eyes, slowly turning them. She was glowing. The illumination stretching out into the night came from her.

Fires spread in the heavens. Now the sky above and the space below her feet looked like the view of a telescope, like a can of glitter had exploded into the night air and hung suspended right there. The pinks, oranges, and yellows of a supernova gathered together. Blues and purples of a distant shaft of radiation flashed in a blinking pattern.

She drifted in space, and instead of the suffocating fear, joy stole through her heart. Lily was gliding on sunbeams. She raised her hands and the luminosity around her swelled. Wow. She lowered her arms, and the horizon started to dim.

Okay, don't do that. Light is good.

The finger that triggered it all continued to shine. She twirled it around her, and it left a streak behind like a Fourth of July sparkler.

This was amazing.

Like a conductor, Lily waved her arms to and fro, and a symphony of radiance responded to her command. Beams shot past her as she gestured where they should go. The night shimmered when she spread her arms and fingers out high above her head.

A hum penetrated her personal firework show. The high-pitched sound whined in the background. Was it almost over? She didn't want to go. The ecstasy of painting with the spectrums of each ray around had banished the terror of the pitch-black that had swallowed her.

She stretched out with her arms extended high above her head. A deep breath calmed her racing heart from the excitement. The Focuser was drawing her away.

One more image from far away shimmered like a mirage in the desert. Her eyes strained to bring it into relief. The stars around changed into lines as she started receding back into the real world. What was that last sight trying to push through?

Another person was out there. A face flickered into view for just a moment. His eyes crinkled with his smile, and a hand stretched out in invitation.

Had she seen the face of Love?

Chapter Nineteen

The squeeze of the helmet released, and the Focuser sat loose on Lily's head. Her eyes fluttered open.

She expected to be blinded by the sheer white of the room. Instead, compared to what she'd just seen, it resembled a dingy t-shirt. Her legs and arms tingled, and she had to shake them out after her psychedelic trip. She slipped the helmet off and turned to find that the hooks had protruded again.

The other girls looked at each other in excitement, but Lily didn't pay attention to the chatter around her. She didn't want to be in the real world—she wanted to create with light. Never before had she experienced such an epiphany. This Focuser must be something, because now she wanted to read and study optics, to figure out the properties and abilities of something she'd taken for granted all her life.

Alexia directed them to the end of the room. Instead of a door sliding open, a panel retracted into the floor. "The Focuser needs to have minimal interruption on the sides of the room. That's why we have the pole and the trap door. It doesn't matter in the ceiling or floor. Plus, isn't it just cool to do something different?"

With that, Alexia took a step and disappeared down the tunnel with a whoop. Belinda directed the other girls down one at a time until only Lily remained. When she stepped to the edge, Belinda held her arm, and her stare bored into the younger girl.

"You're special."

Then she tugged enough that Lily had to drop into the tube. She hit a slide made out of a soft surface that absorbed her fall yet was still slick enough that she careened down and shot out onto a mat in a different room.

What did that mean, she was "special?" What kind of experiences did the others have?

Alexia started talking again. "Okay, here you are in room 9-C. While we're sure you want to talk over the exciting things you experienced, we recommend waiting until your debriefing tomorrow. You may not understand some of the images and feelings. Our specialists will process the brain function readings. Don't worry, everything falls under strict confidentiality for privacy."

Alexia opened the door and they all filtered out into a wide hallway. A coffee bar sat near the entrance to the building. This must be the opposite way from how they'd come in. Another cup of liquid caffeine sounded too good to pass up. She could sip a drink and process the craziness.

She was walking toward it when she noticed Sarah Jane leaning against the side of the hall, her face buried in her hands. The girl's shoulders softly heaved.

"Hey, what's the problem?"

Sarah Jane sniffled and slowly raised her head. A trail of tears, tinted black from her mascara, ran down her cheek. "What did you see with the Focuser?"

"We aren't supposed to talk about it yet, right?" Lily wasn't sure if she could even explain what happened. People would probably think she was on something.

"Never mind. You can't really help."

Lily couldn't leave her like this. She glanced around to see if anyone was paying attention. "At first I was trapped in some black goo. Then I saw some light and the darkness let go. Very crazy. I have no idea what it meant."

Sarah Jane couldn't hold back a sob. Man, whatever got to her was serious.

"Okay, your turn. What did you see?" Lily waited for a few minutes for Sarah Jane to settle down. For a moment it seemed like she would go hysterical.

Finally, it came in a whisper. "I didn't see anything."

"What do you mean? It was supposed to pull something out of us. Go to our core or some psychobabble. You've got to have something."

"You'd think so. I thought I wanted to be a dog trainer or work with animals in some way. I expected to see some happy dogs jumping all over me. Anything. Instead I sat there for the whole time and saw literally nothing."

Lily wondered what the significance was. Everyone else in the room acted like they'd experienced something. She had no clue if it was as immersive as her own battle of darkness and light, but they all seemed excited.

"Maybe there was a glitch, and yours didn't work."

Sarah Jane settled down at the thought. "Do you think that's the reason?"

"Sure. I bet you they didn't have it plugged in, or there was a problem with the wiring. I bet if you ask, they'll get you in again."

She laughed. "Excuse me, your fancy machine malfunctioned with me. Can I go again?"

"Why not? You're paying for this. Err, never mind on that last point."

The two girls giggled.

"Come on. I'll buy you a latte. That will help you feel better."

Sarah Jane picked up a napkin and blew her nose. When she wiped her face free of tears, she missed the mascara streaks down her cheeks. "I don't really drink coffee. What should I have?"

A smirk slipped onto Lily's face despite her best attempt to hold it in. "We'd better start you off slow. Only a double-shot this time."

"A double? Wouldn't a single be better?"

Lily waved a hand in the air. "Shoot, you won't even feel that. It'll be like drinking brown water. No, you need to get a little bang for your buck." They ducked into the line and she ordered for the both of them. A hazelnut mocha sounded good this time, and Sarah Jane went along with it. They stepped outside and carefully sipped their grande cups.

Lily looked at her watch. She had a few minutes before she had to find her next spot. They found a seat amid some café-style tables on a patio to the side of the doors and relaxed in the fresh air.

The sun caught her eye. Lily had always needed sunglasses, being sensitive to the brightness outside. Like a dork, she'd forgotten them at home. Now, somehow, she didn't need them at all. In fact, she could look at the sun without it hurting her eyes or creating a spot in her vision. The sun was a big nuclear reaction—a light factory. Appreciation of that flowed over her. How incredible.

Sarah Jane snapped her fingers. "You don't want to go blind, do you?"

"Huh? No, you're right." Lily shook her head, getting the magic of sunlight out of her mind.

"What do you have next?"

"I think it's media testing. They want to see how well we get around on computers and social media. Really? It's a bunch of teenagers. I bet we can show *them* a thing or two."

"If you do that sort of thing." Sarah Jane looked down again.

"You don't do Flare?"

"Nope."

"Facebook, Twitter? Wait, you're probably more of a Snap-chat girl."

"No. If you don't put yourself out there, they can't make fun of you."

Lily caught a loose strand of hair and twirled it around her finger. "Have you been bullied online?"

A pause lingered in the summer air. "Yes."

A sigh escaped Lily's mouth. Why did people have to be so mean and hurtful? Just because they hide behind a keyboard or screen didn't make their words any less damaging.

"Hey, I know what that's like. When my mom and brother died, people said horrible things behind my back. Friends—

or so-called friends—they were the worst. I know it hurt me. I'm still fighting the depression, the darkness. You can't let them win. You stand strong, if for no other reason than to prove them wrong."

Sarah Jane's eyes watered, but she held her tears in check. "Thanks. I'm sorry about your family. What happened?"

Shoot. Lily had really opened that door, didn't she? Well, she had to talk about it at some point. There was a good chance she'd never see Sarah Jane after this weekend.

An alarm beeped. Her phone.

Sarah Jane's phone beeped too. She reached down and fished it out of her pocket. It was the Alturas app, announcing the next segment.

"I'll have to catch you later on that. We'll talk, okay?" Lily said.

"That will be good. And Lily? Thanks. You've made a difference for me this weekend."

The girls parted ways. Lily didn't expect to help someone like Sarah Jane this weekend. Maybe talking to someone who'd been through similar junk online would help.

Lily glanced up at the sun again on her way to the next building. If anything, the day seemed brighter.

Chapter Twenty

Demarcus took another bite of his apple as he headed for his next appointment. The session on social media blew his mind with some of the behind-the-scenes action involved with Flare. He could start to see how this conference would impact the world.

His ears pricked up, as if he'd just heard his name. Hard to tell over the crunch of his apple. He glanced around to find the source.

John waved at him from a nearby building. Demarcus jogged over to the steps and took them two at a time to get up to the custodian.

"Come in, quickly." John grabbed his arm and pulled him in with impressive strength.

"I'm glad to see you. I know it's not after lunch, but I need your help," John said.

They walked down the hallway. Demarcus checked out rooms as they passed. "Wait a sec, is this a lab area?"

"Yes. They don't have as many researchers due to the conference, and there's a gathering going on right now in the meeting room at the end of the hall. We only have a few minutes." John hustled with a slight limp in his gait, but he moved well overall, despite his appearance.

"Soo, what do we only have a few minutes for?"

They moved to room 12-P, next to John's cleaning cart, and Demarcus looked through the glass slit in the door. It looked like a neat freak and a tornado resided together as research partners: on one side sat nice piles of papers, instruments organized on shelves, and an uncluttered computer area. On the other side, things lay scattered haphazardly across the workspace.

"What's in here?" Demarcus asked.

John scanned both ways. "I need to find out what is really going on behind this conference. I told you my concern that all is not what it seems, yes?"

"Yeah …"

"I believe some answers lie within this room. If I am caught rifling through papers, then I will lose my opportunity. However, what if I caused a diversion?"

"Hold up." Demarcus held up his hand and eyed John. "You want me to grab some papers or snoop around in a restricted lab? I don't know. If you're on a mission from God, then why would you do something like this?"

John rested his hand on Demarcus's shoulder. "My dear boy, that is a wonderful question. I know it looks questionable. However, I believe safety and the greater good is at stake. All I am looking for is information. If I discover that Alturas is innocent, then all is well. If I can find leads pointing to another group using Alturas, then I can do something."

His piercing gaze bore into Demarcus. "However, if there are evil designs behind this conference, then who will do something about it? Will you?"

Whoa. This dude was serious.

"What do you need me to do?"

John entered the room first. He pushed his cleaning cart through the door, then brought in a ladder as well. Demarcus waited for John's signal that he was supposed to enter. He cast a nervous glance down the hall. No other teens were here, so he probably wasn't supposed to be either.

Three knocks sounded from within. He opened the door and slipped inside. John stood on the ladder in the far corner, cleaning a window.

"What are you doing up there?"

"I'm blocking the camera. And getting a cobweb. Look through that pile of papers on the neat desk and see if you can find anything that seems out of place."

Demarcus walked over to the workstation. By the time school finished for the year, he'd noticed that he wasn't just running faster, he could also read quicker and still retain information. "Okay. What does 'out of place' look like?"

John closed his eyes. Was he praying?

"Look for words like 'amplify' or 'nullify.' Or anything that references the Launch Conference. I would think that is out of place in here."

Acting like a spy sure seemed weird. But how strange, considering he'd been invited to such a conference, all expenses paid? Other kids having supernatural abilities, like Harry's wild ability? Something didn't sit right about Rosa either. It made sense to make sure nothing out of line was happening here. Maybe something was going on.

Demarcus double-checked the position of the camera. John had chosen his spot well.

He grabbed the first pile. The papers followed an order according to the table of contents. He skimmed the table and looked for targeted information there. Nothing came up. The pages flipped by and he got a good glimpse of the text.

Too bad he didn't have a photographic memory, too.

Three piles later, he had scanned all the pages on the neat side. He carefully kept the documents in order and set them back where he found them. The dude working here seemed meticulous enough to notice if something was out of place.

"How's it coming, Demarcus?" John called.

"One side down. I need to go over the messy desk now."

"Perfect. Except that the meeting is scheduled to get out in five minutes. We need to hurry."

No pressure, then. Where to start? A half-eaten taco sat over one report. No pattern here, just a bunch of random piles and loose papers scattered. How would he go through all of this?

Maybe it would be easier. The messy dude didn't have a specific order like his partner.

He worked from one side down the other. Nothing seemed terribly important. A lot of techno jargon blurred past. He didn't see any no sinister plans.

Wait. One report had extra taco sauce on it. Lots of greasy fingerprints. That meant it was used a lot, right?

A beeping sound came from John. He took his phone from his overalls and silenced the alarm. "The meeting's over in one minute. We've got to go."

"Hang on. I have a feeling this one's significant."

Demarcus skimmed the table of contents. The Launch Conference agenda. Final plans for the Source. Dates for the transference. Technical specs.

This looked important.

"I found something."

"Set it on the counter. See if you can get out of here before they exit the meeting. I will meet with you after lunch like we agreed. Hurry."

Demarcus couldn't argue with that. It would disappoint Mama so much if he was sent home from the conference for being where he shouldn't be. He hurried over to the door and peeked out. No one that he could see.

The door swung open into a quiet hallway. Empty in either direction. He'd already run over Simon, but the situation called for one more burst. He flew down the hallway and hit the exit.

His phone beeped just as he hit the fresh air. Snap. The Alturas app signaled that he was due for his interview over at 10-D. If he could use his speed, he'd make it without a problem. Except with staff and teens milling about, he'd have to do it the slow way.

Demarcus hopped down the stairs and jogged slowly toward his destination. He hoped that his little espionage bit had been the right thing to do. John sure appeared sincere and trustworthy. But how much did Demarcus really know about him?

On the flip side, what was a "transference"?

John folded his ladder and set it by the door. *Lord, may Demarcus have peace that what he did was for your purpose.* He could sense the conflict stirring inside Demarcus. It wasn't easy to ask him to participate in some deception, even for a really good cause.

He pushed his cleaning cart over to the door. The report Demarcus identified was a mess. John picked it up and skimmed the first page. Indeed, the boy had found something.

He turned to his cart and stashed the report under a package of toilet paper. He'd read it away from the electronic surveillance and return it during lunchtime. However, time had slipped away, and he'd best complete the rest of his rounds.

As he turned, a small black device in a plastic package fell off of a cluttered pile in front of him. He bent to pick it up, and a familiar sense pricked his spirit. *This was important.* The packaging read "Router Strength Scanner." For the sake of the cameras, John pretended to return it to the counter by some other equipment, however, he palmed it and slipped it into his pocket instead. He'd investigate it as well before returning it.

John pushed the cart out the door and loaded the ladder as people left the conference room, led by Simon Mazor. John hadn't met him, but his picture was prominent in all of the marketing for Alturas.

Simon walked with purpose toward him, flanked by a tall man with a goatee and a shorter brunette. The two assistants stayed a step behind and seemed intent on pleasing their boss.

John started pushing his cart toward the bathrooms. He had a job to do, after all, and he would do it well. As he passed Simon, he couldn't help a slight gasp.

Darkness shrouded Simon. Not something visible, but John's spirit sensed a black chain around Simon, squeezing life from him.

And yet there was something promising, too. Simon possessed immense gifting. The Lord had a plan for Simon Mazor.

How had the Enemy corrupted such a talent?

John's spirit grieved for the lost executive as he posted his "cleaning in progress" sign. Simon needed his prayers, and John could intercede as he cleaned porcelain.

Chapter Twenty-One

No time to process the subterfuge that had just happened. Demarcus had to keep it cool and get through his interview. He forced the doors open with a slam and hustled down the hall, looking left and right to find his destination. There, on the right. He caught the knob and pushed through the door.

A lone man sat in one of the two chairs, looking at his smartphone. A look of annoyance flickered across his face, and then he switched to the Alturas smile. He stood and offered his hand. Demarcus put his shades away and gave him a firm shake.

"You must be Demarcus Bennett. I'm Jacob Davis."

"Sorry. I apologize for being late."

Jacob cocked his head. The Alturas rep sat down and switched from his phone to a tablet—fitting for a Silicon Valley company, where everyone was geared up to the hilt.

Jacob motioned to the chairs and Demarcus froze. A device with wires sat on a small table behind the chair. What on earth was that thing?

"Uh, I didn't know there was gonna be a lie detector during this deal."

Jacob gave more of a smirk than a smile. "It's not quite like that. We're not trying to catch you in a lie. That's what a normal polygraph does. This helps us sense what truly matters to you." He pointed to a small refrigerator in the corner. "There are water bottles if you get thirsty. Are you ready?"

Demarcus shuffled to the fridge for a water and guzzled a mouthful. He tried to remember what the bad guys did in the movies to defeat one of these things. Not that he considered himself a bad guy.

He sat down and Jacob hooked him up to the machine. *Think, man. Think. How are you going to beat this if they ask some crazy questions?*

Jacob got settled and fixed eye contact with Demarcus. "The different groups are alternating through some screening activities today to build up a profile, and from there we'll work on unleashing the potential here. This is the basic interview. We'll go through some questions for a little while."

This didn't sound too bad. Demarcus shrugged, trying to act cool. "Sure. Can I eat my apple while we talk?"

Jacob shook his head with his eyes narrowed. So, the dude was a stickler and Demarcus already had a negative with being late. And his distraction idea didn't fly.

"Your responses will be transcribed by the tablet here, so just speak clearly and we'll knock this out."

Demarcus rubbed his palms on his jeans.

"What do you consider your greatest achievement?"

Demarcus mentally offered a prayer asking for forgiveness before responding. "I won the most improved award for the freshman football team." Safe answer. Breaking the land speed record might be suspicious.

"What is your idea of perfect happiness?"

Demarcus's eyebrows raised. Not what he expected. "Let's see. I think it's more than having the coolest stuff or tons of money. I think you have to be doing something meaningful that helps others. I guess if you can do that with someone you love, that would be the ultimate."

"What is your current state of mind?"

Is hungry an acceptable answer? "I guess curious. There's … a lot going on and I'm wondering how it will all play out."

Jacob tapped at the screen. "What is your most treasured possession?"

"Hmm. I think it would be my great-grandfather's Bible. He survived the Pacific theater of World War II with it, and it's been handed down through my family to me. It's pretty cool."

The Alturas rep nodded and fiddled with his tablet again, frowning. "Oo-kay. Hmm. Now, what is your favorite journey?"

Where these not the answers he was looking for? Demarcus scratched the back of his hand, fingering an old scar from when a cat bite got infected and it had to be surgically cleaned out. "My favorite journey? I haven't been too many places. I like it when I get to go surfing on the coast. Maybe it would be the time we went to the Switchfoot Bro-Am. The band has a surfing clinic and then ends the night with a concert. That rocked."

He couldn't help shaking his dreads thinking of the pounding guitars and drums after a day of pounding waves.

"Interesting. What is your most marked characteristic?"

"Speed" bounced on the tip of his tongue, despite his best attempt at holding it back. *No, don't go there.* "People think my dreads are cool."

Jacob looked up. "Sorry. I mean personality characteristic. Not a physical one."

"Gotcha. Hopefully people think I'm fun. I feel cheerful most the time, so I try to spread some joy and humor around."

The interviewer smiled, a plastic grin on his insincere face. Most of the Alturas people were cool, but this guy smelled like a phony.

"What is it you most dislike?"

Probably rude to say "fake Jakes." "I don't like when people are greedy and take more than they need. My mom and I haven't ever had a lot, and we don't sweat it. Too many problems happen when people want more than they can use."

"What is your greatest fear?"

So this was a psychotherapy session more than an interview.

"I'd hate to lose my mom. I've never had a dad, and no brothers or sisters, so she's my rock. That would be very hard." Despite his misgivings about Jacob, it seemed he couldn't help but share truthfully.

"What is your greatest extravagance?"

That was easy. "Shoes."

Jacob stopped staring at the screen and looked up. "That's it?"

"That's all, Holmes."

He poked at the tablet again, his brow furrowed at something on the screen. What did he say wrong? "Which living person do you most despise?"

That question slugged him in the gut. A wave of anger spread over him. Demarcus didn't know how to answer the question, because he didn't know if his father was still alive or not. His mother had endured in dire straits, and his dad wasn't man enough to step up and do the right thing. If his dad was still alive, that would be the fastest answer all day.

"Why do you have to ask that?"

Jacob patted him on the knee in a patronizing gesture. "Don't worry. In the paperwork we had a non-disclosure agreement. This will all be confidential. The psychological profile we put together after today will help us find the best setting for you and your potential, so please try to be honest with us. It will only benefit you."

Demarcus sighed. "My father. If he's still alive."

"What is your greatest regret?"

And this is where it gets complicated. "Not knowing my dad."

He looked around the room, hoping Jacob wouldn't press any further. The stylish, futuristic theme of Alturas continued everywhere, from the dorms to the cafeteria to this room. Built-in monitors in the wall stared blankly down at him. Speakers extended out of the ceiling.

Up in the corner a strange boxy structure with two antennae stuck out. It had the torch logo of the company on it. He recalled seeing it in his dorm room, and he'd seen a couple more hanging at the top of the amphitheater at the opening. Must be some kind of router or modem, allowing Internet connections throughout the campus.

How long did this have to go? Demarcus noticed his foot bouncing like he usually did when he was impatient. The problem was, it was flapping so fast it almost appeared like it was standing still. He slowed it down and glanced at Jacob, who focused like a laser on the tablet.

Jacob kept coming with the questions. "What talent would you most like to have?"

He couldn't keep a smirk from his face. Being an athlete, he always wanted to get stronger and faster. What a trip to have this new gift from God. What else could he ask for?

There was something, though. "I've always wanted to be able to draw. I get cool ideas in my head that I can't get out on paper. I've tried, but I can't get things to look the way I want."

Jacob nodded absently. Demarcus got the feeling the dude was checking out a bit.

"What is the quality you most admire in a man?"

That sounded weird coming from another guy. He guessed it should be the best quality a guy should have. "Self-sacrifice. Being a man means knowing when you need to lay it on the line for others."

Jacob shifted as he adjusted his collar. "Okay, so what is the quality you most like in a woman?"

Blah, blah, blah. Demarcus thought about all of the times his mom talked to him about inner beauty and what that meant. He'd seen it with hot-looking girls who were nasty on the inside and just ripped guys' hearts out. Then there were the girls who didn't have all the looks but had such inner beauty. So, what did that mean to him?

"Caring. Having that compassion or empathy for others."

Jacob's arms stretched out. "Sorry, I get tight sitting here. We've got a few more and we're done. On what occasions do you lie?"

Did he seriously just ask that? How about right now? Demarcus's foot revved up super-fast as he tried to maintain a poker face. "I try not to lie. I think integrity is important. I think I lie most to protect my reputation or make myself look good."

"What's a word or phrase you most overuse?"

"Maybe 'dude.' I don't know."

"If you could change one thing about yourself, what would it be?"

"That's a hard one. I'm practically perfect. Just kidding. Maybe it would be knowing when to joke and when to be serious."

Jacob sat up straighter. "Here's my favorite one. What's your motto?"

Motto? Who has one of those? Other than Jacob, here. "Um, maybe 'all for one and one for all?'"

"You mean you're one of the Three Musketeers?"

"Okay. It's more like, 'you can't control others, but you can control how you'll respond to them.'"

Jacob wrapped his fingers together and did the old finger-cracking trick. "Last one. You're doing great. This one's a doozy though. How would you like to die?"

Demarcus thought about some of his other answers. How he placed such importance on self-sacrifice. He hated how his father hadn't shown responsibility or consideration for him or his mom. About his newfound abilities and the idea that had been tickling his brain about being a hero.

"Sacrificially. Giving my life for someone else, or for a greater cause."

Jacob shot him a wide-eyed look. "Really? Wow, uh. Actually, I was looking for something like heart attack, drowning, etc."

"Oh." Demarcus's cheeks flushed at the mistake. "I think maybe going fast and crashing is my destiny."

Jacob flashed a confused look at him.

Moron. Demarcus had been coy this whole time, and he goes and blows it. "I love the racing video games where you get to bash up your car. My mom is scared to let me drive." Hopefully that would be a good cover.

The rep swiped at the tablet a few times, punched in a few more things, and then powered it off. "Thanks, Demarcus. I appreciate your patience. It was great getting to know more about you. I got some interesting readings."

"You did? Like what?" Totally busted.

"Just that you're even-keeled—the most I've ever seen. Nothing seemed to ruffle you. Usually a question will push some kind of a button along the way." Jacob rose and offered his hand. "You're all set for your next appointment. Good luck with everything this weekend."

Wow. How did he manage that? Demarcus gave him a solid handshake but was glad to get away from the guy. He left the room and slipped another apple out of his bag. He started down the stairs when he was greeted by a familiar voice.

"Did you tell them the truth?"

Chapter Twenty-Two

Demarcus turned to see John's wizened face. "Oh, hey."

John hurried over to him and gripped his arm. For his age he sure moved quick. That limp from earlier had disappeared. And man, his grip was solid.

John looked around. The hallway was silent for the moment. "Did you come from the interview?"

"Yes, sir."

John pulled Demarcus out the doors and down the sidewalk. "Did you tell them about your gift?"

"No, I didn't say anything. Some of their questions probed a little too close, but I kept it quiet. Well, a few of my answers veered toward things. Like a hint. Nothing direct."

John nodded, a contemplative look on his face. "That's good. There is a chance they got what they need. I did some digging in the report you found. Their questions are targeted and leading. And there's a new problem I discovered."

As they walked, John put a hand on Demarcus's shoulder and pointed at an emergency post near the front of the campus.

Attached to the post was a black router. "See those? They amplify things."

Demarcus shrugged. "Yeah, this is a tech company. They have great Wi-Fi."

Now John gave his shoulder a shake. "That's what they look like. They actually amplify a power that suggests and subtly influences everyone around."

"Are you telling me they do mind control here?"

"No. Not like that. It doesn't directly control them. The signal feeds self-worth and inflates it. The people affected feel larger-than-life. Then, by encouraging the ego, it also nudges people in the right direction. There's a strange power here, and it gets amplified across the campus by these boxes."

Demarcus eyed him.

John glanced around. "We should not be talking about this here, though. And did you get to talk to Harry about last night? I feel terrible that he was so put off about it."

"No, we woke up late and ran out to the cafeteria. And we still missed breakfast." His stomach rumbled. "I don't know what he's thinking."

John pulled out a cell phone and looked at the screen. "It's 10:45. What time do you have to be at your next activity?"

The notification for the Launch Conference sat on his home screen. "Says I'm supposed to be in the lab at 11-M in Golden Hall at 11:00."

They came to the fountain at the front and sat along the edge of the cement. A light spray from the fountain tickled his arm as the water bubbled along the massive orb. He scanned the way they came. It seemed that a lot of the attendees had broken out of their sessions and were exploring and meeting up with each other.

John leaned in close. "The fountain should be enough cover for us to speak freely. I believe that they have surveillance equipment all around, so we do need to be careful with what we say."

Demarcus wondered how well the water could cover things up. There weren't too many other options, though, so it was worth a shot.

"Okay, I need some things explained for me. I mean, I get that they'd have cameras and things on their own property. What's the deal with the amplifiers? What's going on there? And how did you find out about them?"

A flick of John's wrist revealed a small black sensor. "I found this in the lab after you left. Some sort of sensor. They're tied to the routers placed around campus." He pushed the sensor and only one bar lit out of four. "This is a weak spot."

Demarcus's mind roiled in confusion. He rubbed his elbow where the road rash still stung lightly. "What does this mean?"

"I do not know the source of the influence, but there is a subtle pull on people that both builds them up and draws them in. It wins their loyalty."

"Dude, I've played video games like that. You increase the character's charisma and you can get sweeter deals from the merchants. Once I talked a guy out of his space hound because I got a bonus on charisma."

John shot a quick glare at him before returning his attention to the device. "This is on the electronic television game, yes? And you think this is a game?"

"Err, no. I don't think so. Anyway, Alturas does good things, so this isn't so bad, is it?"

"I do not think it is good. The Enemy wants to build up our pride, make us think we can do things without our Creator, and he continuously tries to draw people away from our Lord. This is too close to that for me. Anyway, I was called here for a reason, so I know that there are great stakes."

"So, where do you come from, John?" It occurred to Demarcus that he hadn't asked many questions of his own yet. Should he automatically accept what John was talking about just because he brought God up? And who was the Enemy?

He closed his eyes for a moment. "Yes, it is good for you to test the spirits. Even me. Just make sure you do it for all around you, even at this marvelous-seeming event Alturas is putting on."

Demarcus's jaw about hit his lap. "Can you read thoughts? Is that your power?"

John laughed, a throaty sound that rattled in his chest. "No, young Demarcus. I assure you my only power is in my faith and through the grace of God. That doesn't mean the Spirit doesn't speak to me, though."

A couple of Alturas interns walked by, deep in conversation. Demarcus and John paused for a minute to let them pass. Thank-fully they didn't question an elderly janitor and a black kid sitting for a chat.

"To answer your question, I have 'been around,' as youth say now. I most recently came from Greece. The important thing today, though, is that I have been sent here. Meeting you is not an accident.

"Nor is it an accident what is happening to Harry. If you can encourage him that his teleporting is a gift and will be something he will learn to control in time, it will be a big help. I know God is gifting certain people for such a time as this. Keep reading the Bible. There are great stories in there that will be a comfort and guide for you in this. I believe you are like Elijah, to give you some place to start."

"Are we gonna be facing down evil priests?"

"I do not think it will quite be like that. But we must pre-pare ourselves for battle—that much is certain. I believe we must locate at least one more anointed here to stand against the coming darkness."

Impending darkness? Demarcus's heart flip-flopped in his chest. What did this old guy want?

"Um, what exactly do you mean when you say 'coming darkness'?"

John closed his eyes. His lips moved without uttering a sound. *Okay, maybe this guy is crazy.* Demarcus glanced around for an exit strategy.

John didn't open his eyes when he spoke. "I know it sounds inconceivable. However, what would you say at the chance to glorify God with your gift of speed?"

Demarcus sighed. He'd help people. His nature led him to jump into the fray. And he always had the sense God had given him this for a reason.

Grey eyes searched his face. "Have I frightened you off, or are you willing to trust me for one more day?"

Chapter Twenty-Three

Lunch couldn't come sooner. Demarcus patted his belly. *Don't worry, you'll be fed soon.*

His head careened in a whirlwind of confusion. Even though he didn't know John from Adam, the old man's sage words rang true inside. Despite the craziness behind it all.

Still, there was so much cool stuff going on here.

The last session had weird helmets in a room only accessible by a fireman's pole. The device showed your inner passion. Demarcus saw himself in different situations, always moving. Strangely, speed wasn't involved. But he was always busy, helping people.

What would happen next?

He searched for his roomie. He hadn't seen Harry since their failed attempt at breakfast. Hopefully he'd had a good morning. And didn't teleport away. That would be embarrassing.

A stream of people formed into lines for the cafeteria. Demarcus found himself behind the blonde girl who'd taken his picture yesterday. What was her name? So much happened since then it got lost in the jumble.

She glanced back and recognized him. "Hey. Need a photographer again?"

D'oh. Here he was fumbling for her name, and she'd turned to talk to him.

"Nah, I'm good for now. Thanks, though. How's the conference going for you?"

She glanced at the ceiling as if the answer was written up there. "I'd say it's been … enlightening. How about for you?" He caught a twinkle in her eye with her answer.

The truth wanted to jump out of his throat. *Oh, you know, I came here with super speed and met a teleporting roommate, plus an old Middle-Eastern dude is talking conspiracy theories with me.* That probably wasn't the best plan. Better think of something fast.

"It's cool." That was the best he could do? He gave himself a mental forehead smack. What was it with this girl with her deep blue eyes?

"Ah, 'cool.'" She made air quotes. "Well, I hope you keep having a good time. And don't forget to send those pics home."

He had actually forgotten to do that since the excitement last night. He made a mental note as he tried to keep the conversation going.

"So … what was so enlightening for you? Did you do the focus-y thingy?"

Blondie giggled and his heart stuttered.

Think, man. What was her name?

She wagged her finger at him. "Uh-uh. We're not supposed to talk about it. Especially not in the lunch line."

"Demarcus?"

His name carried down the hallway. They'd almost made it through the doors into the cafeteria proper, so he had to lean out of line to see who called his name. Harry scanned the crowd anxiously. Demarcus waved his hand, and Harry dodged the others to skid next to him.

"What's going on? Can I jump in line with you?"

The people right behind them continued their own busy chatter. They probably wouldn't mind. "Sure."

Harry sidled up next to him and stopped, gawking at the girl. *Great. The guy's never seen a cute blonde before.*

She shifted a step back. "Um, what's your friend's name?"

Demarcus slapped his hand on Harry's chest. "This is Harry. He doesn't get out much."

Harry shot him a wounded look.

"Oh, and this is ..." Awesome. His brain still couldn't click.

The girl offered her hand. "I'm Lily. Nice to meet you, Harry. I'm glad Demarcus here could introduce you."

Ouch.

Harry found his tongue. "Hey, Lily. Where are you from?"

"Originally, the Seattle area, but I moved to Palo Alto a year ago. How about you?"

He ran his fingers over his gelled hair. "Kinda the same. I just moved a few months ago from Kalispell. It's in northern Montana. Ever hear of Glacier National Park?"

She shook her head, and strands of her light hair fluttered around her shoulders.

"Too bad. It's amazing up there. Almost as pretty as you." Harry immediately flashed red across his whole face. "No. I mean, it is beautiful up there. I didn't mean …" He groaned and bit his knuckles.

Poor guy was going down in flames. What was the line from the fighter pilot movie? Crash and burn.

Lily smiled sweetly. "It is okay. A girl likes a compliment. At least I made an impression on you." She said the last bit with her eyelids narrowed, a subtle glare aimed at Demarcus instead.

Not cool. Harry makes points for being awkward, and forgetting her name gets him in the doghouse.

This time they'd hit the trays for the lunch line. The three of them grabbed their utensils and plates and surveyed the options. The smell of sizzling beef wafted by, followed by a tangy tomato sauce from pizza, which gave way to the fried goodness of onion rings.

The food took Demarcus's mind off of Lily's burn. She chose a Caesar chicken salad while Harry went for the fish sticks and fries.

Juicy beef patties with black streaks from the grill called to Demarcus like a siren. He picked out one with a slice of orange cheddar dripping off the edge and loaded it with the works. He finished off the plate with some of the golden onion rings and green beans with bits of bacon in them. Had to get his bacon fix somehow. A carton of milk completed the meal nicely.

Lily joined another blondish girl at the table and Harry tagged along mindlessly. She waved to the empty seats, so Demarcus joined them.

"Sarah Jane, this is Harry and—" She paused for a moment. "—Demarcus, I believe."

Point taken.

"Harry's just moved from Montana."

Sarah Jane waved a fry in their general direction. "Where are you from, Demarcus?"

"Seems like we're all transplants. I'm in San Jose now, but I used to live in San Diego. How about you?"

"Originally from Phoenix. We must be the weird table, because my family relocated here, too, last September."

"They weren't kidding when they said we were from all over. Can you imagine all the work it took to find us?"

Harry surveyed the kids sitting down and still getting their food. "I still can't figure out why they chose us. I mean, I don't feel like I belong at all. What about you guys?"

Lily's gaze darted, scanning the cafeteria. "You know, I haven't had a chance to meet anyone other than you and I haven't figured out a connection either." She stopped and stared at Harry's plate. "And what in the name of sanity are you doing with your food?"

His head jutted up, the fish stick in his hand dipped in some sort of yellow yogurt or pudding. "What? It's fish fingers and custard. Well, I'm not sure if this is custard, but it's close."

Demarcus wanted to gag, and the girls had horrified looks on their faces. "Why would you do that?"

"It's from *Doctor Who*. Have you heard of the show?"

Lily and Sarah Jane shook their heads, lips curled in disgust. Demarcus had only heard the name before, nothing else.

"Wow. It's only the best show in the world. It's from England, and in one episode he needed to eat—"

Everyone turned a little green at the thought.

"Aw, never mind." He bit the custard end off and started eating them normally after that. The group slowly returned to their own food in silence.

Demarcus noted the other kids around the lunchroom. A good bit of diversity peppered the cafeteria. Some tall, some short. Some were stylish like Lily, while others fit the nerdy stereotype. As he scanned the room, he saw Rosa chatting up a Japanese kid, batting her eyes at him. No singular physical trait or ethnicity defined the attendees. It must be something mental or some aspect of personality that drove the screening process.

Seeing Rosa reminded him of her earlier disappearing act and rekindled his curiosity. What if everyone here had some kind of power? After all, he had his speed. Harry did whatever it was he did.

He considered the girls in front of him. What could it be that made Lily and Sarah Jane special? His imagination conjured up some goofy power sets and names. He had to concentrate to keep from laughing out loud.

Sarah Jane peeked at him. "What's so funny?"

"I was just wondering what would happen if we … started a food fight," Demarcus said.

They all looked around at potential targets. Lily shook her head. "Yeah, that probably wouldn't go over well with them funding everything."

Okay, he'd dodged one. He started to take his last bite of burger when he noticed something in the window behind Lily.

John gestured toward Harry and pointed to outside, then he held up one finger. Take Harry outside when they were done and meet at one o'clock? He could do that. He needed to just swap numbers with John instead of meeting in weird places.

"Whatcha staring at?" Lily swung her head around. Clear skies and green foliage peeked through the window.

"Um, nothing really."

She gave him a suspicious look. Now he looked like a space case.

So, where did John go?

Chapter Twenty-Four

Pulling Harry away from the girls proved harder than Demarcus had expected it would be. Dude was emboldened by how well Lily took to his compliment. Demarcus couldn't blame him for running with a good thing.

They had a half-hour before John asked to meet them. Demarcus still fought his confusion over John's accusations about Alturas, and Harry needed to hear more about their gifts. Hopefully, if they met with John, they could get more answers.

Teens spilled out onto a central lawn area they called the Quad. Trees dotted parts of the rectangle to provide shade, but there was plenty of open room as well. Some kind of pavilion sat in the center.

The day was beautiful, with a slight breeze providing just the right amount of cool to compliment the warm sunshine. Someone broke out a Frisbee and started tossing it around. Demarcus had to restrain himself from jumping into the midst of the action.

Instead he led Harry to a quiet, deserted area of the campus, away from the main areas where the other attendees hung around. Harry trailed behind him. "Man, what are we trying to do? What's so important that we had to leave the girls?"

"I told you, we have someone that wants to meet with us." Demarcus led him around to the far side of a quiet building. "First, I have an idea."

They turned the corner. No one was there. Perfect.

"What's your bright idea?" Harry said.

Demarcus put an arm around Harry. "When my speed started manifesting, I wasn't scared by it. I kept pushing it, seeing how fast I could go. Have you done that?"

"Why would I do that? All it's done is cause me problems. Shoot, last night it could have killed me. I want it to go away."

They stopped. Demarcus stepped in front of Harry and flexed his arms. "That's exactly my point. If you're going to use a muscle, you have to train it. Let's see if you can control it. How wicked would that be?"

Harry frowned. "If I could control it? That would be great. The problem is I don't have a clue about how to do it."

This might be harder than Demarcus thought. He wracked his brain on motivational speeches he'd heard from coaches before. "Dig in deep, man. Find the … thing in you that makes it work. How do you feel when it comes on?"

A bird flew above, a song trilling from its beak. Harry almost ducked at the sudden sound. He scratched behind his ear, definitely trying to delay things. "I can't tell. My body gets a quiver—it's like the first drop on a roller coaster. Except it's not consistent."

Okay, that's a start. "How do you feel right now?"

"Full."

Demarcus smacked his forehead. "Let's see if you can focus on something. There's a spot over there—see that cement pad by the bush near the building? No one's around. See if you can teleport over there."

Harry scrunched his face. His fists balled. And nothing happened.

One eye opened. "Am I still here?"

"Nothing at all. So, you can't pick up anything that would help you guide this?"

A breath of frustration escaped Harry's lips. "Dude, I told you. This freaks me out. I can't imagine trying to make it happen. Sure, the idea has some potential. I guess I could be first in line when the new game comes out to Game Depot."

This guy was hopeless. He couldn't see the value of popping up wherever he needed to be? Well, Harry did have scary consequences from his ability glitching. Hopefully he'd find out how to get a handle on it soon.

They still had time before meeting with John. Demarcus needed to redeem himself in Lily's eyes. Forgetting her name did not set well with either her or him.

"C'mon. Let's go see if we can find the girls," Demarcus said.

That brought a spring to Harry's step. Demarcus led the way around the corner of the building. What luck. Lily and Sarah Jane sauntered down the pathway, away from them. It'd be a snap to catch up.

He spun back to his friend. Harry had gone quiet, and he didn't look good. His red hair set off his pale face. Harry twitched a little.

"Oh, no. Why would it happen now?" His green eyes stood out in a mask of panic.

Wait—it wouldn't come on when they were trying, but now, around all these people? A quick scan didn't show anyone around. For all Demarcus knew, Harry might just appear in the midst of the crowd on the Quad. Or in the fountain.

Well, that would be kind of funny.

Demarcus jogged over and pulled him behind the cover of the building. "Dude, are you sure it's going to happen?"

Harry went rigid as if trying to will himself to stay there. "It doesn't always happen when I feel like this, but I always feel like this when it happens."

"Grab on to me. I bet you'll stay here."

"No!"

He tried to dodge. Demarcus got a firm grip on Harry's arm to reassure him.

Then the universe turned upside down.

Chapter Twenty-Five

Demarcus couldn't see straight. His vision swirled around and he stumbled backwards.

Harry laid a hand on his back. "Are you all right, Demarcus?"

"I don't think so …" Demarcus slumped to his knees and proceeded to empty the contents of his stomach at the base of a tree. So much for lunch.

"That was an answer to prayer."

When Demarcus looked up, John strode toward them. "Heaven's mercy! Are you well, Demarcus?"

His head had stopped swimming for the most part. "What just happened?"

Harry stepped forward, his head hung low. "I happened. I blinked out again. That's what happened to me the first few times I teleported. You get used to it, though."

John knelt down between them, offering a handkerchief. Demarcus took it and swiped the excess saliva and grime away from his mouth. That was not an experience he wanted to repeat.

"Wait a second. Do you mean we just transported from one area to another?"

Harry nodded. "Yeah, we did. I don't recognize this spot. There's no one around except John. I didn't know that it would work to take someone with me."

Demarcus wanted to be impressed. Really. His stomach being left behind consumed his thoughts instead.

John took his cloth and folded it into his pocket, despite the nasty souvenir Demarcus left on it. "Let's move over to this bench and talk."

The trio moved over the stone bench with Demarcus leaning on Harry to get there. That teleport trip was a doozy.

John beamed. "Harry, that was incredible. I've not heard of that in many, many years."

"You've seen someone do it before?" he answered as he raised an eyebrow.

"Not firsthand. Are you familiar with the book of Acts?"

"Can't say that I am."

"Well, there was a man called Philip. A real man of God, willing to do whatever was asked of him to spread the gospel. He was traveling on a road and found an Ethiopian official who was reading the Old Testament. Philip rode with him and shared about Jesus. They stopped at a river so the official could be baptized. When Philip finished, he was taken in the Spirit to another town, miles away."

Demarcus felt his stomach start to relax again. That story did sound familiar. He'd never really thought about Philip actually teleporting somewhere. Now, though, it made sense.

Harry tapped his temples a few times. "Okay, I'm trying to get my head around this. You're saying that a biblical dude did the same type of thing I'm doing. This is like … a miracle?"

"Precisely. You are a smart lad."

Harry bit his lip. "I don't get it. You're saying this is a gift from God. Right? But this terrifies me. I don't know when it will strike. I can't control it, and I end up in crazy places. One time I ended up in a tree. And what about the middle of traffic last night? How can that be something from God?" His hands shook with his confession.

John didn't speak. He merely sat and let Harry process, with a fatherly gaze trained on Harry the whole time. The only sound for a minute was that of the birds chirping in the nearby tree.

Demarcus watched with a twinge in his heart while he tried to sit upright without swaying.

John patted Harry's back. "There is a mystery in God's ways, and I cannot explain it all. However, I have been around long enough to trust that there is a good purpose behind his gifts. There will be a time when it is made clear to you.

"Just look at right now. I asked Demarcus to bring you to meet me so we could talk again, except my old brain did not give him a location. So where do you end up? Right by me. Even with you dropping into the street, it brought you two closer together because you now share in this. Have faith, my young friend. It will work out for the best."

Demarcus slapped his knee. "Besides, dude, you gotta be pretty tough to handle that. I don't wanna do that again anytime soon. Ugh."

Harry stood up. "Look, I don't know about this miracle stuff, but no one's ever treated me like that before. So, thanks. And if you have more information about this, I'm willing to listen."

John clapped his worn hands together. "Right. I believe you both have been chosen. There is something going on, and it will require gifts of a supernatural variety to stand against the attack. Like I said, I think there are more of you here. I have yet to find anyone else."

Demarcus had been meaning to ask about Rosa. "Do you think everyone here has some sort of power?"

"I do not believe so. That would be remarkable, but I do not think there will be fifty individuals. Still, Alturas has done fascinating work in drawing in the youth here."

Both boys clamored to speak. Demarcus stopped to let Harry go first. "That's the biggest question: why are we all here? We were all so excited to get invited initially. Now everyone wonders what criteria were to be chosen."

John leaned in. "I am an old man and not very good with the technology. But God has grace for me, and I am honing in on a theory. Let me do some more checking on my idea."

Demarcus stood up and stretched, finally feeling like his body would work properly. "What do you think about the Focusers?"

He shook his head. "That is something I can't investigate directly. That room is on lockdown, even for my clearance. There is very little to go on. What was your experience?"

"It was a trip, for sure."

John scrunched his bushy white brow. "I did not think you left the conference for this."

Harry couldn't suppress a laugh.

"No, I mean it was a really different experience," Demarcus said. "Not as strange as a ride on the Harry Express here, but the way you perceive everything in front of you is incredible. Funny thing—there wasn't anything about speed with me."

John scratched his chin. "I have overheard a few things, rumors mostly. I am very curious and concerned about how the Focuser does its job. Harry, have you done it yet?"

Harry looked at his phone. "Shoot, that's where I'm supposed to be in a few minutes. We have to go. Sorry."

"No, that is quite all right. You boys go and take some notes for me if you can. Will you meet me after dinner tonight to speak again?"

Demarcus whipped out his phone to check the app. "It will have to be later. There's a party at 7 p.m."

The elder nodded in agreement. "You both need to have some social experience here. I believe God is orchestrating occurrences, and coincidences are not what they seem. Yet keep your eyes on the Lord. A lot that transpires here is not apparent on the surface."

All heads turned as Simon clapped his hands and rubbed them together, the friction heating his excitement. "Okay, ladies and gentlemen. What updates do you have for me?"

Screens flickered around the room with images of teens in different locations around Alturas. The dorm rooms were off limits, but the team had agreed the myriad of cameras in buildings and around campus ought to be enough.

A state-of-the-art facility needed security, right?

Simon paced the room, surveying the different views offered him. Kelsey stayed at his elbow, tablet at the ready.

One image caught his attention. A custodian blocked the view of one of the main project labs. Why would he do that? Simon almost called for Kelsey to make a note to check things when the man lowered out of view, and Simon spied a rag in his hand. Okay, he was a thorough cleaner.

Nice to have such dedicated staff, even in a custodial position.

When the view opened up he saw the custodian clean up a bunch of wrappers left at a station. Who was the researcher responsible for such a mess?

"Kelsey, find out who left their garbage in the lab. Terminate them."

"Sir? Do you want to remove someone when Flare 2.0 is so close?"

He turned, a snarl on his face. "I want people to understand their place." Kelsey hunched her shoulders and took a step back, tapping furiously on the tablet.

Otto squinted at one view behind the support center. "What is it? Anything interesting?" Simon walked over behind his giant operations manager. He rarely felt small, but standing next to Otto dwarfed him.

"Isn't this the boy we checked on earlier? The one with speed?" Otto pointed to a still showing two boys facing each other.

"The one with dreads. After our last run-in, I definitely won't forget him."

"Watch this."

Otto tapped on the screen and the image moved in real time. The speedster grabbed the other boy. Then they disappeared.

"Okay, we knew he was fast …"

Otto showed some figures he'd calculated on his tablet. "If this is correct, the kid is the fastest thing ever seen on land. I slowed the camera down. It isn't high definition so I can't do an exact measurement. Still, he had to go screaming to move out of frame that fast."

Simon tapped his fingers against his pocket, his mouth watering for a gummy bear. "It will be amazing to see what he can do tomorrow."

A vibration from his pocket alerted him to his next appointment. "Great job, everyone. Keep the observations up. I don't want to miss a thing."

Chapter Twenty-Six

The crowd filed into the amphitheater, the energy palpable. Goosebumps percolated on Lily's skin with all of the excitement pinging off of everyone.

By this time, all of the attendees had visited each of the day's stations. Nothing had been as invigorating as the Focuser. Now that Simon was coming in to address them again, the day was shining brightly again.

Except for a thin black mesh stretched over the open seating to protect everyone from the California rays. Lily didn't know why that annoyed her, but it did. Let the sun in. Why dampen its beauty?

Sarah Jane stopped in the middle of the row, and the two girls sat down. They sat closer to the stage now since both of them had made a point to get in line early for that very purpose. Lily blushed when she realized that mostly girls populated the front of the line.

The guys brought up the rear. She glanced behind, scanned the crowd, and easily picked out Harry and Demarcus—the spiky redhead sitting next to the guy in dreadlocks. They appeared deep in conversation so they didn't see her. Must be talking about some important man stuff.

She also spied Missy chatting up some tall blond guy farther back. *Run, dude, while you still can.* Lily couldn't resist a chuckle at the thought. At least the poor boy had provided a focus for Missy and kept her off Lily's case.

An elbow tapped her arm, and Lily turned.

"I've heard that Simon isn't dating anyone right now. He broke up with that actress, Shannon Dye." Sarah Jane wagged her eyebrows at the statement.

"I'm sixteen. I think I'm too young to have a chance with him."

Sarah Jane shrugged. "I just turned seventeen, and he's only twenty-four. Who's to say what could happen? Maybe he likes mousy girls with ridiculously pale complexions."

Lily gave her a side hug. "Hey, don't believe that crap. You are lovely, inside and out. See what those bullies do? They get you buying into their lies."

Interesting how well Lily could give out the advice she had problems accepting herself.

Brooke Stephens, her counselor in Washington, had been helping Lily claw out of the abyss after the accident. If only Dad hadn't chosen to move right then so he could cope. Maybe the last year wouldn't have been such a black mess.

The sound system fired up with a pulsating string section. The pyrotechnics didn't flare to life today, and the build-up didn't last long. Simon strode out on stage wearing his checkered shirt with the cuffs rolled up.

The cheers and shrieks from the audience around her hurt Lily's ears. Normally, she would've thought it all too much. Hero worship wasn't her style. But the genius entrepreneur didn't have to host an all-expenses paid conference for a bunch of teens.

And his hotness factor didn't hurt.

A screen lowered behind Simon as he tried to calm the group down. It still took a few minutes for everyone to quiet themselves. He pointed to the small wireless mic along the side of his cheek. Message received.

"Hello to the future, here. How's the conference so far?"

The whooping and hollering picked up again. Lily couldn't help herself.

Simon waved the crowd silent again. "This is so awesome. I've got to tell you, people thought I was crazy to bring fifty teenagers here. Especially when I said they were going to change the world. Boy, you guys are already proving them all wrong."

The conference erupted again.

Simon quickly shushed them, waving his arms like an umpire calling a runner out. "Listen, there's so much potential bursting inside all of you. Do you want to know what we found with the Focuser sessions?"

A chorus of "yes" rang out.

"Well, I can't tell you tonight. Tomorrow we're going to put you in groups of five. These have been specifically crafted to maximize what we can do this weekend. Ten different teams, working on influencing your peers and making a change in the world. I can't tell you when I've been more excited.

"There are more surprises yet to come. First, I want to show you this video clip." He stepped back to the screen and pulled a laser pointer out of his pocket.

Lily watched the little red dot flit around the screen as he started to explain. That was a puny light. Surely he could do better.

The red dot flared in intensity. Even in the daylight, the beam shone bright, cutting through the air to the screen.

Simon froze, shaking and tapping the device for a moment.

Lily's eyes widened. *What just happened? How ... did that light do that?*

Simon turned to scan the crowd with a grin on his face. Now a video of a ship on the ocean appeared on the screen. The waves lifted the vessel up and down as a boom stretched out from the stern of the boat with a long, snake-like tube in its grip.

"This is the latest fiber-optic technology. How many of you enjoy your smartphones? Your tablets? Streaming movies and music, chatting with friends, sharing pictures?"

All the hands shot up with more adulation.

"I would hope so. That's what Flare is all about, after all. It's all made possible by these tiny filaments that shoot digital signals across the globe. From Hong Kong to San Francisco, London to Johannesburg, this is what connects our world. If you have a good fiber optic network, then you don't have problems with dropped signals, poor connections, and all of the other modern-day problems with technology."

He flashed the bright light around the cable getting lowered into the water. "This is a live feed from the final line Alturas is installing in the Pacific. When this is turned on, our world will be joined together like never before. We've been carefully setting up the fastest, strongest network on the planet. A fleet has been laying these down across oceans and deserts to link us as a whole species.

"The final preparations are in place. But this is a secret. I'm sharing this with you as an exclusive, because you're part of this. When we launch the new Flare, the world will change. That's why we brought you here. You will be a vanguard to go out and show the youth of the world what can be done when we are unified."

The video abruptly stopped, and the screen retracted. Simon strode to the front of the stage.

"And I for one can't wait."

With that, he tossed the pointer into the crowd and walked off the stage.

Hands shot up to catch the token, clamoring for a souvenir from Simon.

It landed in Lily's lap.

Chapter Twenty-Seven

Lily fished through her suitcase. The party started in a half hour, and she had nothing to wear. A pile of skirts, shorts, and pants lay across her bed along with an array of different shirts. But she had nothing. She'd stared at her options for the last forty-five minutes, while Sarah Jane had left to call home. Since the presentation this afternoon, she wrestled with how to get ready.

Kelly had packed extra for her. The idea of a dance switched on all of Lily's anxieties, which made her want to default to the all-black look again. However, the stepmonster had insisted on her being able to dress stylishly. *It's only appropriate for such a special opportunity,* she'd said.

It probably was the closest she'd get to Simon, so why not try to dress her best? Lily sighed and plopped on the bed.

Something poked her in the back. She flipped over and found the laser pointer. The sleek, silver metal felt cool to the touch. It looked like a miniature pen with a couple of buttons rising from the side.

She rolled over again and aimed it at the ceiling. When it had hit Lily's lap, a miniature scuffle had broken out with the girl next to her. Lily managed to wrest it away before it escalated further. Sarah Jane's eyes widened at the tenacity Lily showed in hanging on to it.

The best part was when Missy walked by and sniffed in jealousy after everyone else had cleared out.

Now she clicked the button, and the red beam shot out of the end, a little dot wiggling up on the ceiling. It wasn't very strong. The other switch must make it brighter, like the difference she saw on stage.

She clicked that one. This time the light became a strobe, flickering in the room.

She hopped off the bed, killed the overhead light, and pulled the slick white curtains closed. The lack of sunlight dimmed the room considerably. Kicking back on the bed, she turned her new toy on again.

The beam visualized better, but it still didn't shine very brightly. That was strange. It had significantly changed in intensity when she thought about it needing to be brighter during Simon's talk. She tapped it like he did.

The dorm room blazed with a luminous red glow.

Lily sat up, examining the gadget as the laser spilled out in front of her. This little gizmo was amazing.

A strange scent wafted through the air. She sniffed. Was that smoke?

She raised her head. Where the beam struck a spot on the curtain, the material had turned black and started smoldering.

A shriek escaped her lips, and she dropped the laser. The room darkened. She grabbed the glass of water by her bed stand and doused the singed curtain.

Her chest heaved with deep breaths. She didn't think those type of tools had enough juice to trigger a fire. Why would Simon toss out such a powerful laser?

Where did it go? She'd better find it and turn it in or something. At least not leave it lying around. But with the curtains drawn and the light off, she couldn't see in the darkness. She needed some light.

Instantly the room brightened.

Lily spun around the room, taking everything in. The light switch was still off. The window was still blocked by the slightly damaged curtain. Where was the light coming from?

Her hand. She held it up in front of her face. Her skin gleamed. It couldn't be.

What was going on?

She walked in front of the mirror. Her whole body glowed, and the glass reflected the glare around the room.

She waved her hand in the air. A starburst flared with the motion.

No—turn it off.

She lowered her hands and retreated to the corner of the room. The illumination stopped, plunging everything into darkness.

The pounding in her chest hurt. Breaths came in ragged gulps. Her skin prickled all over with a pins-and-needles sensation. The hand she'd just waved tingled the most. She shook it out, but the sensation persisted.

Thoughts careened within her skull. This was incredible. It was crazy. It freaked her out.

Sweat broke out on her brow, and her stomach started twisting deep within. Tremors rippled from her core, splaying out to every inch.

What. Am. I?

The darkness seemed to creep in toward her. Her gaze darted around the room. She couldn't handle the darkness again. Even though the idea of light scared her, she wished for it to brighten.

The lights in the ceiling didn't turn on. Instead the room slowly increased with incandescence. Again, the glow radiated from her.

Lily covered her face with her hands. The vision from earlier trickled back to her. Something like a voice whispered in her mind.

"You were meant for this. What does your name mean? Lily stands for white and purity. Beausoliel is French for 'good sun.' This is no accident. You were meant to illuminate the world, to show the way."

Who was in her head? Where did those thoughts come from? What way was she supposed to show?

This was insane. A few weeks ago, she wanted to be engulfed in darkness, and now the total opposite manifested in her? How did this happen?

Was she bitten by a radioactive lightning bug?

A soft knock sounded through the door. She leapt up, wiggling her fingers. How did she shut it off? Maybe the light from outside would do something. She threw open the curtains.

"Lily, are you ready for the party?" Sarah Jane's voice carried into the room.

"Just a second." Lily closed her eyes and squeezed them tight. No light. No light.

Her eyelids popped open. Nothing radiated from her. The tingling returned, but she didn't look like a glowworm. Okay, take a breath. Calm down. Pretend like you're not a human flashlight.

She pulled the door open slowly. Sarah Jane stood in front of her wearing a pink tank top with flowing ruffles and some yellow shorts. Freckles dotted her skin all over. Lily knew Sarah Jane felt insecure about her looks. Lily couldn't see why, because she looked really cute.

Sarah Jane walked in. "I didn't want to walk in if you weren't decent. Oh—you're going like that?"

Oh, yeah. Lily had been trying on clothes before she started the room of fire and turned into a night light. Her jean shorts and t-shirt combo wasn't very fetching.

Sarah Jane surveyed the clothes strewn across the bed. "All of this and you can't find something to wear?"

Lily shook her head. "My stepmom packed for me. Trust me, I would've packed a simple wardrobe if she'd let me."

"Well, you can't let some of this go to waste." Sarah Jane picked up a polka-dotted skirt. "We've got to get going. Let me pick for you if you're not in the mood."

Lily shrugged. Why not? She still had palpitations from her unexpected light show. But as Sarah Jane played dress up with her, a thought formed in her head. What could she do with this crazy … thing?

Chapter Twenty-Eight

Demarcus strolled through the crowd of kids, taking in the sights. Harry tagged along beside him, playing wingman. He passed by a couple of the guys he recognized from his focusing group. "Hey Bruce, Jim. How's it going?"

They raised their cups at him and continued with their back-and-forth arguing. Those guys always seemed to be debating something.

Demarcus hit the edge of the crowd and stopped to take in the sights. This was a separate pavilion that they hadn't been in before in the center of the Quad. It was a recessed cement square with curved edges and stairs on each of the four sides. It reminded him of a skateboard park without the ramps and rails.

On the north and south ends, scaffolding held speakers on each corner, blaring out top-forty tunes with thumping beats. Light canisters hung through the middle, shining various colors down along the ground. He felt like they were inside a prism.

Harry checked things out as well. "They do put on a good party here, don't they? This is awesome." He sighed. "If I feel a trip coming on, I'm going to bolt, so please just try to cover for me, okay?"

Demarcus slapped his shoulder. "I got your back, bro. Don't worry, though. It's out of your system for the day, right?"

"I don't know, man. It's so crazy unpredictable."

"Well, quit talking about it in public. Comic book rule, remember?"

Harry wasn't answering. He was staring. Demarcus followed his gaze.

Sarah Jane and Lily approached from the direction of the girls' dorm. Most everyone was dressed for a party tonight, but the girls stood out from the people coming through the Quad.

It was more than their clothes—skirts and tank tops in place of the casual shorts and shirts they'd worn earlier. Something about them, about Lily in particular, seemed to glow.

Demarcus shook himself out of the haze enough to see that other guys had taken notice as well.

And these girls came right up to Harry and him.

Demarcus ran a hand through his dreads. "Hey."

Not much, but Harry had nothing.

"Hey, guys. How's the party?" Sarah Jane twirled slowly, taking it in with a beaming smile. She was usually the quiet one.

Lily glanced around, her hands fidgeting with curls in her hair.

Harry gulped. "Better now that you're here."

Smooth recovery, bro.

"Otherwise it's a party. Pretty cool set-up though, right?" Demarcus pointed out all the tricks on the scaffolding. Sarah Jane clapped her hands and hopped, a squeal escaping her lips. Lily only scanned the perimeter quickly and kept her head down.

If something was bothering Lily, could he help her in some way? They barely knew each other, so he didn't know how to reach out. Still, the four shared a bond in the short time together. Something drew him to his three new friends, a cord pulling him into their orbit that he couldn't explain.

The crowd of teenagers and the college-aged staffers from Alturas wandered the pavilion in a slow, circular pattern. The refreshment table acted as a watering hole, a gathering place for different small groups to join up and break off in new configurations.

Demarcus and his three friends managed to stay together as a pack, even though different guys made attempts at pulling the girls away. Flirty banter and showing off occurred regularly, yet Lily and Sarah Jane kept their distance and seemed content with their company. Demarcus wasn't sure why they shared this connection. Still, he wasn't going to complain.

The sun set in the west, elongating strings of light stretching in the sky, retreating from the coming night. Now the light set-up really dazzled. Demarcus hadn't noticed a curtain hanging from one of the scaffolds. The music scratched to a stop and the party hushed. Everyone looked around to see what was going on.

The black material parted, revealing a table of electronic gizmos. A DJ with a ball cap askew and black wrap-around shades with a neon border scampered out on the stage area.

"What's up, gang?" the DJ yelled into the mic. "This party needs some ramping up, and here to get us started is the man to do it." He stepped back to allow Simon to approach the mic.

"Hey gang. The night is young, and you guys need to relax and enjoy the party. I've invited a friend to stop by and say hi." He swept his arms to the side as a lithe woman in a sequined top and shorts scampered out. "Ladies and gentlemen, allow me to introduce Tia Torrenté."

The four of them shared an astonished look. He didn't! Demarcus shouted over the din, "I can't believe he knows Tia!"

The pop star wrapped Simon in a tight hug and waved to the crowd. "Hey, guys! I'm excited to be here. Simon says you're the brightest around. That's so cool." She flipped her long dark tresses away from her face. "I'm pumped to celebrate with you."

The crowd cheered, and she blew kisses around the pavilion.

"Thanks. Simon asked a favor from me. Who wants a sneak peek at my upcoming single? It's going to be a Flare exclusive release next week!"

Demarcus leaned over to Harry. "Pinch me, dude."

Harry did.

"Ow! Hey."

Harry raised an eyebrow. "You asked."

How cool to have his favorite new singer here. As the teens chanted Tia's name, a Latin beat thumped out of the speakers. Tia whipped her hair around, did a few salsa moves, then grabbed the mic stand. Her lilting voice belted out the lyrics while she swayed with the beat.

This conference rocked.

Everyone pulled their phones out and began snapping pictures. Flare's servers must've been burning up with all the posts. Demarcus thought of his friends following him online.

Sure enough, his phone started blowing up with comments and likes.

The music ended with two thumping beats, punctuated by hip shakes from Tia. The cheers threatened to break Demarcus's eardrums, but he joined right in anyway.

Tia's porcelain smile shone as she caught her breath. "Thank you, Launch! This was so much fun. Listen to Simon. He's been instrumental in my career taking off."

With that, Simon stepped beside her. She planted a kiss on his cheek and bounded off the stage, waving as she disappeared.

Simon took the mic. "Did you like that?"

Another cacophony of cheers erupted.

"There's a lot to do this weekend and we've only started. So, let your hair down and pretend you've known each other forever. Get the energy going. It's only going to take off from here! Be a light!"

Demarcus joined in the chants of "Simon." Staffers handed out long, thin glow sticks, and everyone started wearing them as bracelets or linking them together to make necklaces. The DJ hit the turntable and kicked the tempo up with the music. The crowd started to let loose again.

Kids hit the middle of the pavilion and broke out their best dance moves. Amateurs. Demarcus didn't see anyone killing it out there. Time to step up and show what he could do.

He handed his cup to Harry and gave his friends a wink. A lanky kid was doing a passable robot-type dance. Demarcus hopped into the center of the floor and started slowly. His hands and feet moved in unison as he popped and locked to find his rhythm. A few people started cheering in the background.

Time to show off his flexibility. He dropped to the ground and bent back at an extreme angle, doing the Matrix move, his shoulders now touching the ground. A voice called out. "Yeah, whatcha gonna to do now?"

Demarcus pulled himself up to face the robot kid. Robot's eyes narrowed and he stepped right up to Demarcus's face. He jerked away and dropped to the ground, doing a few breaking moves, hands and feet alternating on the ground and flashing into the air. He ended with a backspin, sliding to a stop with his chin on his fist. Robot nodded his head once, and Demarcus got the message.

"You top that?"

A chant broke out: "Dance, dance." Demarcus winked at the robot dude and started with a simple groove, swaying and swinging his arms, letting the music flow through him. The driving beat fed the beast within. He slipped into some glide moves, sliding around the floor, making it look like he floated over the ground.

Robot stood up and waved dismissively at Demarcus's moves.

Demarcus took a quick couple of steps towards Robot, who ducked back. Then Demarcus flipped backwards. The people around roared at that. He spun into a high kick directly on landing.

Robot's eyes grew large and his puffed-out chest deflated in defeat. He bowed his head and spread his arms out in front of him, ceding the floor to the rightful winner.

Man, I should totally bust out my speed and wow the crowd. That would blow them away. A grin broke out as he spun on his heels, prepared to crank it up a notch.

Something caught in the corner of his eye. A set of blue work coveralls.

He paused and saw John standing just off the perimeter of all the celebration. John didn't do anything, but something in his eyes and his furrowed brows counseled caution.

Demarcus wrapped up his showboating with a spin on his heels, followed by a split. Applause broke out from the circle that had formed around him. Kids nearby slapped him on the shoulders and congratulated him. He allowed himself a slight bow, then stepped back to allow others to keep the flow going.

Okay, what just came over him? Something had shifted in his brain and overran his inhibition. And almost his common sense, too.

Still, the dancing broke the ice for everyone, and teens swayed and bobbed to the music. Harry, Sarah Jane, and Lily surrounded him, and he led them to the side to catch his breath. He took his drink in a hand-off and guzzled punch.

"Dude, I had no idea you had it in you." Harry slugged his arm. "The only move I can do looks like a drunken giraffe."

Lily wrapped her arms around his shoulder and Harry's. A hint of vanilla and spice filled his nostrils from her perfume. "That was brilliant!"

Sarah Jane completed the circle by joining the other side.

They looked around at each other with knowing looks in their eyes. Then they raised their arms, breaking the loop with a shout. Each of them joined in with the motion of the crowd. Interns and staff members watched from the sides as the teens in the pavilion seethed and writhed like an animal in motion.

At one point Demarcus saw Rosa, her arm wrapped around a different guy from the one she was talking to earlier. The dude spun her around and pulled her back toward him. She had some decent moves as well. When she clung to her partner, she finally made eye contact with Demarcus. Her eyes widened with recognition at first, then she winked and mouthed the words, "Nice moves."

Rosa seemed awfully flirty. Maybe he'd keep his distance.

Demarcus knew better than to let his speed go, but that feeling of release fell over him again when he started dancing with his friends. Harry cut loose with his arms in the air and his head shaking. A drunken giraffe, indeed. Sarah Jane bounced from each leg and tried to match the beat.

And Lily. She swung her arms in the air with a beaming smile on her face. She turned in a slow circle swiveling her hips and keeping her hands up high.

As the night wore on, the light show intensified. The colors almost made Demarcus dizzy with the spinning, flashing, blinking that coursed around the dance floor. And if he wasn't mistaken, the lights always seemed to find Lily.

Not that he minded.

Lily wanted to throw her arms around everyone in the pavilion. The joy overflowed from her like the water erupting from the fountain at the front of the campus.

For the first time in over a year she wasn't weighed down by the burden of her loss. Her mother and brother faded out like wisps of smoke in the recesses of her mind. All she had was right now, this moment, as the youth danced and thronged together.

Her new friends Demarcus, Harry, and, of course, Sarah Jane orbited around each other yet remained anchored as they whirled around the floor. Even the overwhelming confusion and the fear of what had happened earlier in her dorm room melted away like a candle left to burn all night.

Delight pumped through her veins. She should share what she had with everyone, to express her joy and the gift inside. She noticed the spotlights on the scaffolds, smaller versions of the one that almost crushed Clara. They pulsed in a static pattern, and the metal canisters didn't move. It seemed a shame that the lights couldn't dance too.

As Lily twirled, she imagined the lights spinning with her. Soon the various colors swirled around the floor. It was as if she were a human disco ball. The other kids cheered at the special effects.

The DJ waved one arm to the beat as the other worked the turntable. Tia Torrenté swayed in time, her eyes closed. Lily directed some light toward Tia, and the sequins on her outfit reflected a thousand beams across the crowd. Simon just stood next to the star, clapping and watching the proceedings, searching the crowds.

She'd give him something to see. An image dropped into her mind. A large, graceful butterfly, floating on unseen breezes, its wings flapping in time with the sound thumping around her. She slowed her jive to concentrate on the picture in her mind.

It would be simple to do in her photo editing software, but how to do it in real life? A finger. She had used a finger in the Focuser to help draw out the light.

She acted like she was doing a slow dance move and twirled her finger in the air, conceiving a butterfly in flight. A pink outline formed in the air above the dancers, looking like a squiggly cloud of electrified noodles at first.

No, that wasn't what she wanted.

Her eyes narrowed as she focused on the mental pattern. The fuzzy blur sharpened in definition until a bright butterfly flitted about, just above the reach of outstretched hands.

Ooohs and aaahs accompanied the ethereal insect. Harry looked in his drink. "Did they spike this with something?"

Lily laughed. "No, they must be doing a special effect."

While the crowd watched her creation dance, Lily scanned the party. No one seemed to be pointing her out. Good. If they liked the butterfly, what else could she do?

Now that she'd figured the process out, a cascade of holographic forms sprung from her imagination. Lily stopped on the side of the undulating crowd and crafted each one internally. Then she waited for the music to swell, and she skipped back into the throng and flung her arms in the air.

A myriad of swirls, flowers, and sparkles exploded in the air. Fairies and hummingbirds flitted around the light show. The partygoers gave another hurrah, cheering Alturas and the extravagance of the party.

Lily couldn't resist a huge smile as she considered the truth. This was so amazing! She loved sharing her gift with everyone.

And as she pranced around the perimeter, she passed the DJ table where Simon and Tia danced and watched. Simon caught her gaze and smiled widely at her. He raised his hands and clapped.

Lily knew that was for her. Her heart jumped and the tingling from her power magnified even more. The temperature spiked 100 degrees hotter and sweat started trickling down her forehead.

Simon had noticed her.

Chapter Twenty-Nine

The oak doors swung open wide and boomed when they hit the walls behind. A grand night truly deserved a grand entrance.

Simon shuffle-stepped into the room, pumping his fist in victory with each step. His exuberance had no bounds with the night's success.

The conference's progress at this stage was greater than he could have hoped. The teens fawned over him and ate up every morsel he planted along the trail. Which meant the proof of concept held. His gift covered a greater amount of people than just the immediate staff he had contact with. Thanks to the Source, he could broadcast his influence across the campus.

Phase one complete, with phase two well on its way.

The impact worked best on people younger than him. That was one glitch he'd like to work out. But harnessing the power of youth had worked for the Beatles and countless other cults of personality. Simon and his Master would just use his gift to amplify the effect deeper than anyone before them.

He'd started out with nothing. Parents that controlled him and never gave him an opportunity to try anything for himself. Then he found that if he concentrated, people listened to him. He could bring the best out in people, and it seemed to subtly draw them to his perspective. In high school, teachers labeled it a gift.

Funny how things work. At a summer conference before his junior year, the Master had come to him and introduced him to the plans of the Archai. He learned about his gift and began to control his ability, to do something with it.

He sighed in near contentment and sank into a leather chair in the meeting area. His muscles melted into the smooth cushions. What a day.

Of course, he couldn't really relax until he proved that he wouldn't be controlled anymore. He had the ability to influence people to bigger and better things. The possibility of a new world order rising up was within sight. If he was optimistic yesterday, the occurrence at the party only confirmed it.

He pulled his Ziploc bag out of his trousers and decided to splurge on two gummy bears. Orange and white. That was a weird combination. Things could go either way tomorrow based off of that color grouping. Almost like a double-or-nothing bet.

His senior staff members filtered in. Of course, senior was relative. They were all under the age of 25, yet they had worked with him the longest. He trusted them with the day-to-day operations of Alturas and the vision for Flare. It didn't hurt that they shared the longest exposure to his gift. They were wired in at this point.

Their chatter matched his excitement. Good sign. Time to recap the day, pull together all the findings, and filter out the markers that didn't fit the objectives. Simon couldn't wait to hear confirmation for some of his own observations.

The crew, as he liked to call them, sat in a circle. He noticed energy drinks and coffee cups in their hands—drinks of choice after a long day. The smell of roasted coffee beans saturated the air. Good. They'd have focus and drive. He bounced on his cushion in anticipation.

"Okay, everyone. You've all worked hard today to bring out the best in our guests. We'll cut to the chase and go over the readings. To start, Kelsey, do you have the security footage from this morning?"

Kelsey tapped on her tablet, and a video streamed onto the screen above the fireplace. The footage from the cafeteria hallway sped through kids coming and going out of the lunch room. Then a small gap until two boys hurried in. She slowed the video.

Simon, Kelsey, and two others walked down the hall. In a blink, Simon sprawled on the ground, entangled with a dreadlock-headed kid.

Kelsey punched in some new commands. "We need to slow this down more to fully see what happened."

The clip slowed to half-speed. Simon's entourage tracked slowly across the field of vision. Then a figure darted out of the cafeteria and collided with him, and the two ended up in a heap.

Otto stopped stroking his goatee and leaned his tall frame closer. "Wow, that was fast. Have we been able to calculate the speed?"

Kelsey checked her notes. "I consulted with engineering. They estimated about 30 mph when the teen crashed into Simon."

No wonder his back had ached all day.

"We have other footage on him, but this is the best viewpoint to figure out his speed."

Another eager intern, Kate, jumped into the fray. "Do you want us to call him in for discipline for running you down?"

Simon shook his head. "No, I'm not mad at him. I wanted this substantiated. Our screening process picked up some other surprises beyond our prime target. We've got facial ID on him from this, right?"

Jillian Prowse filed through some papers. She always had a preference for dealing with hard copies, despite working for a technology company. "I have it right here. Demarcus Bartlett. Sixteen-year-old who will be a sophomore in the fall. From San Jose."

"Good. Steer him into our high echelon group tomorrow. Any other surprises?"

Simon's best friend on the crew, Jackson Adams, flicked the side of his prototype glasses display. "Here are the results on an intriguing candidate. Harry Wales from Milpitas. Initial findings suggest he's got a latent ability that hasn't manifested yet. The readings on the scans clearly show increased levels on his potentials."

He beamed a photo up to the screen. A redhead with short, spiked hair and a worried face stared back at them.

Simon quietly clicked his fingers, a habit when processing new information. "Do we have identification on what his power is?"

Jackson touched his glasses again, swiping files across the television in rapid fashion. His speed-reading ability could out do the rest of the crew in that department. "We don't. There are variable readings we haven't been able to classify."

"That's okay. Does everyone agree he'll be a candidate for the high group as well?"

The staffers nodded in unison.

Simon clapped his hands and rubbed them together. "Any other findings out there?"

The group brought forward a couple of other high potentials. They debated the readings and placed the kids accordingly. It all excited him, but he patiently waited for the final reveal. The key they needed.

"What about the shining girl?"

Kelsey raised her hand. "We have confirmation. The girl is Lily Beausoliel, recently moved to Palo Alto from Seattle. She fit the basic profile to a tee: wounded with potential. Interestingly, the Focuser found things we've never seen before. She's a light-wielder. Levels went off the scale. In fact, we recalibrated the headset afterward to be sure."

"How many of you were at the party tonight?"

A-ha. Everyone shared looks, averting their eyes from Simon's. Finally, Jackson spoke up. "We were busy collecting and analyzing all of the data."

Simon stood up and walked the room. "We have to remember to not get so focused on the numbers and graphs and information that we miss the observations right in front of us."

He slipped his phone out and twirled it in his hand, then he swiped to open Flare. A video streamed to the screen.

The images flickered and took a moment to orientate. The DJ's music mixed with the cheers of the party. Teenagers jiggled around under the lights, which sometimes flashed so brightly it whited out the view. An amorphous glow hovered above the crowd until it formed into a pink butterfly that flew and bobbed over the teens' outstretched hands.

Simon smiled at the stunned silence of his leaders. The same way he had felt earlier in the night.

The last image showed an eruption of light sculptures, and the camera zoomed in on a blonde girl with her arms raised high.

Kelsey looked at her screen. "Yes, that's the girl. She did all that? The analysis indicated it wasn't fully activated yet, much less that she had that much control."

Simon sat down on the couch and leaned forward, intently waiting for the answer he needed. "She's the one that Flare 2.0 needs. Is she going to be able to do this?"

Kelsey fiddled with her tablet. "I don't envy her last two years. Her mother apparently had a drug problem that resulted in a car crash killing her and a younger brother. Then her father remarried, and they moved to Palo Alto for a new job. She's also struggled fitting in at school."

How could he measure the worth of his research team? With these details, Simon should have no problem influencing Lily. And yet, the detail of an alleged drug problem lodged in his mind. Why was there a question about there being a drug problem?

Jackson's eyes flicked around behind his specs, analyzing the screen. "Everything on our testing suggests she will. The question is if the strain will be too much for her."

Everyone shifted their gazes to Simon. He stood up. "With all we've strived to do, it will be a small sacrifice."

Chapter Thirty

Demarcus was in heaven. He finally got his bacon, and he popped a piece into his mouth while winding through the food line. The crunch released the smoky flavor into his mouth. Now if he could avoid being teleported, he could hold it down.

Mixed feelings swirled in his gut. The party last night was such a blast. From a slow start, it had exploded in energy and fun once Simon kicked it off. It felt good to let loose with some of his dance moves. The action had continued late into the night, and he felt a bit drained today.

The staff had shut it down at 11pm to keep them from going too long. They needed to be ready for the excitement today.

Despite his fatigue, the rest of the cafeteria was charged up. Alturas would reveal the action groups after breakfast. Everyone wanted to know whom they'd be working with and what the groups would do.

Still, he kept having the thought that no one really knew what the outcome of the weekend would be. The words sounded inspiring, but what did it all mean? He couldn't point to anything concrete announced at the conference so far.

Another feeling, that he'd forgotten something last night, nagged at him.

His arm bumped against someone when he turned from the line. "Dude. My bad," he managed through the rest of his bacon.

A Hispanic girl looked up at him. "Don't worry, it takes more than a tap to knock me over."

He almost choked. "Rosa Gonzales?"

Her eyes narrowed. She scanned his face. "Wait. Did we have a class together?"

"Yeah. Computer in 5th hour from Mr. Gordon. Funny running into you here."

A slow smile, like a jungle cat knowing its prey was trapped, parted her lips. "It really is. This is something incredible, isn't it?"

Demarcus nodded, his mind racing about the weird encounter the first night when she disappeared. "I bet the teachers at school would freak if they saw us here."

Now a frown broke out, and her eyes darkened. "Something like that. Anyway, I'll see you around. I've got to meet someone."

Rosa winked at him and wandered back to a table where the guy she had danced with last night looked concerned. Was it that she had talked to another guy? That dude didn't have anything to worry about.

Lily, Sarah Jane, and Harry joined him at the table. Their little group all seemed subdued today. Demarcus couldn't put his finger on it. Everyone had partied hard last night. Was that all it was?

Harry fiddled with his French toast sticks, absently dipping them in applesauce. Not as bad as fish sticks in pudding, but still weird. Even Lily slowly slipped her coffee. She must have done something different with her make-up this morning. Her complexion seemed radiant.

The screen in the cafeteria flickered to life. Simon plunked down in a chair in a faded red shirt with a soda pop logo.

"Hey there, mighty cadets. Who had fun last night?"

The room roared in approval.

"Now begins the critical part of the weekend. After your meal you'll come to Redwood Hall. There will be partitions set up on the lawn next door. We're splitting you up between ten stations. Names will be listed under a number before you enter the area. Find the number and line up according to the order listed.

"You'll be directed to a counselor ready to place you in your functional groups and let you know where you'll meet with them. Then you'll be given your initial meeting time with your group to figure out your agenda. This is where the rubber meets the road, gang. Let's go change the world."

The video blinked out. Just then everyone's bands beeped in unison, and the whole room focused on their wrists. Demarcus's band read "4."

"What did you guys get?"

John wiped down the desk in the headquarters, even as he searched through drawers. He meant to infiltrate and discover the truth about Alturas, yet a compulsion pushed him to do a good job while he was at it. His supervisor had already complimented him on how clean the bathrooms were on his rounds.

Do everything as unto the Lord. Old habits were hard to break.

Nothing here. He needed to find more information on the transference and how Simon affected the youth. John recognized some kind of mind control or influence going on. Simon's gifting? He'd sensed it the other day. Except he couldn't find any information on how it worked or what the ultimate plan was. It was like a black hole.

John's lips moved in silent prayers as he moved into the lab next door. His quality work and favor from above had earned him a badge that allowed access to secure areas, but so far, he'd heard only whispers and rumors from the staff. Not enough to expose the threat of this company or the people behind it.

His most significant find thus far was the discovery of the two boys and their gifts, and the document Demarcus had uncovered helped focus his investigation. It wasn't enough—he needed a breakthrough. The conference continued to progress, and he couldn't let the anointed fall under the sway of its charismatic leader.

Simon Mazor. John kept pondering this wounded young man, who had some gift, something supernatural, beyond the genius that enabled him to build the Flare network.

John spoke in an ancient language, interceding for the anointed, the ones he still needed to find, and for Simon and his staff. They were lost, and they needed light in the worst way.

The lab had multiple workstations topped with the best computer equipment John had ever seen. Papers lay scattered across the surface of the long metallic table along the far wall. He couldn't wait to find Demarcus and do this with a diversion. Alone, he had to risk the surveillance cameras.

He wouldn't have time to get into the computers, and the security likely surpassed his meager technological skills. He could only learn so much, even with grace, at his age. Perhaps the papers held the needed clues.

John worked his way back, trying to maintain his cover as long as he could. Nothing stood out over the computer stations. At the large worktable, he spied a large schematic on blue paper for a spherical metal object. Two large cables protruded from its bottom, as well as four supports, likely to function as a stand.

Technical writing filled the sides of the blueprint. John wiped a rag around the area with one hand and pulled some reading glasses out of his chest pocket. Nothing stood out that he could understand.

A faint, tangy odor caught his attention, even over his cleaning chemicals. He scanned for the source. At the right end of the station, an empty soda cup sat next to a loose packet of hot sauce that leaked red liquid on the metal.

The taco-lover. His poor hygiene may be a gift from heaven. Instead of rushing right to the messy station, he tried to work with deliberate patience. When he reached the mess, he made sure to scrub the table thoroughly, and he tossed the empty containers in his garbage.

What could these other documents give him? He frantically scanned the technical jargon. Wait—something stood out: "Global amplification of the signal will exponentially increase if powered by an appropriate source." The paragraph continued with the mathematical equations to prove the statement.

How could Simon do that? The routers throughout campus amplified his control, but the signal was limited. Even with them sending the message out farther, it weakened at the boundaries of the campus.

John fingered the sensor in his pocket. The little gadget he'd borrowed earlier measured the signal strength. When he used it, he discovered the routers, and it led him to this building.

Something intense would have to spread the transmission worldwide without it degrading. What would that be?

His hand, absently wiping circles on the counter, pushed some papers aside and revealed two small plastic containers in a clear bag. Each one held a circular Band-Aid-type patch with micro circuitry embedded in the center. The label read, *Nullifier*.

Those might come in handy. He pushed the papers back over the spot, but his rag held the Nullifiers. He slipped the bag into his pocket.

Why would anyone need Nullifiers? Was Simon going to use his gift to affect people and broadcast it to the world?

John snapped his fingers. *That's why the fiber optic cables were featured in that rally. He means to send that signal across the globe and hold sway over billions. That sphere on the schematics must be the amplifier. What could possibly power it?*

A beep sounded from his other pocket. He pulled out his cell phone.

It was time.

The boys had failed to show after the party. At least John had gotten the speedster's attention. John had sensed Demarcus was about to expose his gift.

The signal at the party pushed the sensor reading to maximum. It must have clouded their minds, because every teen stopped at the same time and returned immediately to their dorms. John had no chance to catch them afterward.

He had to intercept Demarcus and Harry before their assignments. John needed to warn them of his findings, and, if possible, uncover the power supply for the global plan.

Chapter Thirty-One

All of the Launch attendees made their way toward Redwood Hall. Different groups chattered in excitement on the walk there. Lost in thought, Demarcus trailed a step behind Harry and Sarah Jane, with Lily pushing ahead in anticipation. Despite the collective thrill everyone had about getting their assignments, something didn't sit right with him. And he was pretty sure it wasn't the bacon.

He couldn't explain it, but the closer they walked to the assignment area, the heavier it fell over him, like a dark cloak. Dread was the closest word he could think of. Why did he feel this way?

The attendees split for their separate stations up ahead. As Harry rounded the corner, Demarcus heard his name in a forced whisper. His head snapped to see John, urgently waving him over.

"What's up, John? We have to get over to our assignments." Demarcus pointed toward the outdoor setup.

"I know, son. This is important. I've found more information that something sinister is transpiring. We don't have much time, so let's trade phone numbers so I can reach you later."

Demarcus glanced back to where Harry and Sarah Jane had disappeared and pulled his cell. "Um, okay. Just message me your contact profile. That'll be the fastest way to—"

"Confounded thing. The buttons on my phone are too close together." John fumbled with an older flip phone that had seen better days. A crack distorted the screen and the rough edges revealed plenty of abuse. Demarcus stifled a chuckle at the sight of John playing with his phone. *Wow, which one of these is older, John, or the phone?*

"I'll just punch my number in for you."

He took the phone and tapped away. How did anyone live without a smartphone these days?

While Demarcus fiddled, John pulled out three items from his pocket—two round plastic containers with little patches in them and a small sensor device with a tiny LED screen. "You need to keep these safe. This one is a sensor to detect the amplifier around campus, and the others are some sort of Nullifier. Don't let them out of your possession."

Demarcus swapped gadgets with John and slipped the new items into a pocket in his cargo shorts. "Yeah, I'll keep them. What is all this about? Oh, and we were supposed to meet with you after the party. Man, so sorry."

John shook his head. "Don't worry about that. I'll explain later. I need you boys to keep your wits about you. Remember the old saying, 'if it's too good to be true, it probably is.'"

Before Demarcus could ask another question, two men dressed in black shorts, security shirts, sunglasses, and ball caps came up and bracketed John.

The shorter one on the right spoke first. "Sir, we need you to come with us. There's a security concern we need to discuss with you."

John held his hands out. "I can do that. First may I ask what the problem is, gentlemen?"

The guards didn't wait to answer. They hooked him under his armpits. The taller one on the left said, "You have violated security protocol. You're fired and your pass is revoked. If you cause any further problems, you will be turned over to the police with charges of trespassing."

"May I speak to my manager? I believe there is a misunderstanding."

"No. We have our orders from upper management." The man turned to Demarcus. "Sorry, kid. We're in a hurry."

What on earth was happening? These guys were going to muscle John outta here? Demarcus grabbed the shorter one. "Wait a minute. You gotta take it easy with an old ... I mean an elderly gentleman."

The man grunted and shrugged him off. "Take care of him, will ya?"

The taller guard pulled out a device that looked like a key fob and pointed it at Demarcus.

Demarcus backed off a step with his arms raised. "Hey man. I don't want any trouble."

The guard jerked the fob up next to Demarcus's temple. His body twitched, and a blanket of static fell over him.

What did he need to be doing? Oh, right. Time to get to his assignment.

Harry ran up to him, waving his hand in front of his face. "Are you there?"

Demarcus caught his arm. "Dude, you don't need to do that. What's the deal? Was I staring? Doesn't matter, cause we've got to get over to the assignment place."

"What's going on? Why is John going off with those guys?"

John? That name rang a bell. His mind must be a little fuzzy from the partying last night. What was Harry talking about?

Before Harry could say any more, a couple of Launch staffers called to them. "You guys are the last ones. Come on over. Demarcus, you go to four. Harry is at five."

They jogged over. Demarcus could tell Harry was confused about something, but he couldn't figure out what the big deal was. Too bad they had to split up, although Demarcus would see him again tonight. "Dude, I'll catch you later."

Harry clasped his hand. "You bet. Hey, keep your eyes open. Something weird is going on."

What was the big deal? Demarcus walked over to join his group, shoving his hands in his pockets on the way.

He pulled out three strange objects. Two plastic containers and a small scanner with an LED screen.

Where did these come from?

Chapter Thirty-Two

The cool grass tickled the sides of Lily's feet as the blades rubbed across her sandals. The answers behind the Launch Conference and their invitations awaited them. Finally. She fingered the laser pointer in the pocket of her shorts. The little gadget that had helped reveal her powers would be her good luck charm today.

Her heart leapt at the possibilities.

After experimenting with her abilities last night, her exhilaration threatened to bubble over. At breakfast people talked about the light show amongst the chatter. It didn't sound like anyone had pegged it to her. The thought of their little group breaking up had subdued her emotions, but as they drew near Redwood Hall, excitement powered through her.

The boys and Sarah Jane trailed behind, chatting and laughing. The bond they'd made so soon impressed Lily. Especially Demarcus. His maturity had really impacted her. He had good sense, a wisdom that served him well. It made him so much different than other guys she had known.

The sidewalk opened up to a large circle with different imprints formed into the cement. Palm fronds, swirls, and stars symbolized the Pacific coast and the beauty of the area. She inhaled a deep breath, taking in a little part of California with it. The blast of fresh air awakened her mind even more, a hint of lemon dancing on the breeze.

Maybe it wasn't so bad here.

The line formed at the circle and extended back out of the area. Ten different portable gazebo covers, their sides draped, offered some privacy. Signs on the outside listed the five people assigned to each makeshift cubicle. Lily's band said she was in number seven. She was the last in line for her group, so she turned around to survey the scene.

There was Missy going to number one. Missy turned just then and caught Lily's eye. Lily could make out Missy's sneer from across the way. Hopefully they stayed this far apart for the rest of the conference. Swapping for Sarah Jane as a roommate had been a huge blessing. As they had talked about their experiences of bullying, it helped Lily open up to someone new. Besides Clara, she didn't have many friends since moving.

She noticed Demarcus had been pulled aside by an older guy. He looked like he was a custodian of some kind. They weren't close enough for her to eavesdrop. Demarcus's body language and crinkled face suggested confusion about what the old guy was telling him.

The sun hovered high enough that its rays heated up the outdoor area rapidly. Some of the kids fanned themselves. Lily marveled at the power inherent in every ray of light. Each little beam contained so much, and she could see every wavelength of potential. Science wasn't her strong suit, but she had a feeling if she studied light, she could do more with her strange abilities.

The lines shortened. Lily was next. She glanced behind one more time. Staffers shooed Demarcus and Harry to their places, and the old guy had gone. Demarcus looked like he and Harry were arguing about something. She wondered what the old guy had told them to upset things.

A rustling sounded from the cubicle behind her. She spun around. The divider had fallen down, still swaying in the air. A voice called out, "Next!"

A very familiar voice. One that sent chills scattering through her every nerve fiber.

Lily pulled the curtain back. An open chair sat in front of a small table. Behind the table sat Simon, a Cheshire grin on his face.

Chapter Thirty-Three

L ily stood there, star-struck. The inventor of Flare sat right in front of her, literally only three feet away. Wow. His dimples were even more impressive from this close.

That was a silly thing to think, girl. Get your head on straight.

"Lily Beausoliel?"

Her mouth opened and words didn't form. Shaking her head would work, right? She nodded.

"Hi, Lily. Have a seat."

She floated to the chair and sat down. He extended his hand and they shook.

"How's the conference been for you so far?"

Perfect, now. She couldn't get over how stunning he was in person. His tousled hair framed his strong face. His complexion stood out against the shade of the gazebo.

"Uh, it's been pretty cool. I still can't believe I'm here, honestly. I keep wondering if you guys made a mistake."

Simon laughed deeply. He tapped on a sheet of paper on the table in front of him. "I can promise that you were meant to be here. Don't sell yourself short, Lily. You do not have to do that anymore."

Huh? How did he know? Her eyes widened. Her pulse pounded in her neck.

"I told them I wanted the chance to announce to someone where they'd be assigned. As luck would have it, I get to meet you. It's a real pleasure, Lily. I think this next step will be very illuminating for all of us."

She couldn't help but giggle at the unintended play on words. If only he knew.

He gave her a quizzical smile. "What's the joke?"

The sheets of plastic separating the cubicles weren't exactly soundproof.

"Oh, I'm just pinching myself that I get to meet you. I'm a big fan of your hair. I mean, your social network." Heat rushed to her cheeks, and she wanted to shrink until she could hide in the grass. What a stupid thing to say.

Simon flashed an "aw, shucks" look and winked. His eyes were such a deep brown. Like a rich cup of coffee. "It's okay. When I met my first celebrity I was tongue tied myself. I think I accidentally proposed to Jennifer Lawrence."

Lily found her hands tingling. Was her power going off? No, she was just hyperventilating. Breathe, girl. In, out. Nice and easy.

He shuffled a paper to the top of his pile. "We've got some groups that will work on various projects. Social media. Street team. The brain-stormers will work with the planners and hash out some cool new strategies. Awesome stuff going on."

"Am I in one of those groups?"

Simon leaned in slightly, enough to trigger more palpitations. "No. You may not realize how special you are Lily. I see that you have potential that is vastly untapped. You're going to be in the group that I personally mentor."

She gulped. Her world swirled for a moment, and she gripped the armrests to stay upright.

He chuckled again. "Your ears did not deceive you. Our Focuser and interviews helped identify those teens with truly unique abilities. I want to see you harness your potential and let it out. We're going to meet in room 9-C at the Cove, you and a few others with similar untapped latencies. We're going to see if we can unlock what all of you are truly capable of."

He pushed a button on his cell, and a brunette stepped into the square.

"Kelsey here will take you over. We don't want others getting upset at my hands-on work at the moment, so let's keep this between us. I'll see you in about thirty minutes. You just be ready to shine."

Lily wasn't sure how her feet managed to move, yet she seemed to be walking alongside Kelsey, the assistant. Lily's thoughts swirled like the rays of sunlight streaming through the sky. How was all of this—the conference, meeting Simon—even real?

Yeah, if Simon wanted, she could shine. Shine like the sun.

Chapter Thirty-Four

Demarcus left Redwood Hall, ready to join his new group. A small headache throbbed behind his eyes. It had come on right before he got his assignment. He shook his head, dreads flopping, as he tried to clear his mind. He hadn't gained any more insight on what they'd be doing. The sheet just read: "Target Group." Whatever that meant.

The directions led him deep into the Alturas campus. He hadn't been this far back before. He walked past a couple of office complexes and approached a large, gleaming structure. The Cove.

The large columns up front gave it a classical architecture appearance, but the large glass windows and sharp lines marked it as modern as well. His mouth gaped as he climbed the steps.

"Demarcus?"

He swiveled to find Harry behind a column, leaning against the massive pillar. "What are you doing here?"

Harry brought over his own sheet. Yep, it read 9-C. They were in the same group.

"That's sweet, dude." Demarcus high-fived him. "I can't believe we get to stick together." He had to wonder though: were they in the same group because of their abilities?

Harry squinted at him and cocked his head. "Man, are you sure you're okay?"

Demarcus cuffed him on the shoulder. "Yeah, it's all good. Let's go see what we're doing."

Harry stood a few inches shorter, yet he gripped Demarcus's shoulders and gave him a firm shake. "Don't you even remember what happened to John? Those security guards were dragging him off."

John. The name rang a bell. Oh, the old guy that … had warned them about weird things going on. "Security took him away?"

"Are you kidding me?" Harry smacked his forehead and gestured back to Redwood Hall. "You were right there. Didn't you see it?"

"Are you sure you're okay? I don't remember that."

Harry looked up at him, his green eyes ablaze with serious-ness. "Dude, we need to be cautious here. Question everything. Remember that if it's too good to be true, it probably is. We need to dig into what happened to John after our session, okay?"

Their Wi-Fi bands both beeped, and a countdown from five minutes started. Demarcus nodded as they entered the building. He wasn't sure where their confusion came from. If he could find John, that would calm Harry down.

The bit about things being too good to be true, that resonated within him. That was advice his mom always gave him. It seemed like he'd just heard someone else saying it too.

The glass doors closed behind them. The two boys looked at each other, and Harry's eyes widened. Inside, an expansive leather sectional faced a fireplace, and an ornate wooden coffee table occupied the middle of the room.

However, that wasn't what Demarcus saw when he approached the glass front of the building. He turned to examine the wall. Instead of an expansive view of the campus, a tropical scene of palm trees swaying and waves rolling placed them in a beach house.

He pulled the door open. No, they were still on campus. He walked outside a few steps. From here the glass shone crystal clear, showing a vestibule leading to a wide staircase. Except that's not what he found inside when he ducked back in.

"Have you ever seen anything like this?"

Harry shook his head. "Nuh-huh."

Simon entered from a hallway. "It's holographic glass. I enjoy the view here, but sometimes I want to see something else. Here's the surf rolling in on the North Shore of Oahu. Even if I don't have a different vista up, it works as a one-way mirror so you really don't see what happens in here. Not bad, right gentlemen?"

Demarcus nodded. "Epic. Sir."

Simon laughed. "Call me Simon. Come on in. Oh, wait a second. Here's the last person from your group that I'm expecting." The tropical image faded enough to see a young woman skip up the steps.

"Motion sensors trigger and show me who's approaching." Simon explained.

The door opened and Demarcus's jaw dropped in shock. Rosa entered, her petite frame dwarfed by the large room. She carried her shoulders high and strode in with confidence. She took in the surroundings with the same expression that Demarcus and Harry had a minute ago—one of awe.

"Is this where you want me? They told me to come here."

Simon stepped forward and extended his hand. "Rosa Gonzalez, I assume?"

Rosa took his hand. She looked him over once with a raised eyebrow. "Yeah, that's me. And you're Simon Mazor?"

He flashed the megawatt smile from his promotional materials. "That's right. Welcome to the target group."

Rosa did a slow spin to take everything in. She twirled as she gawked at the tropical hologram. Her eyes finally fell on Demarcus. "Hey, you. Fancy seeing you here."

What the heck? If Rosa was here with Harry and him, then she must have something going down. When she'd disappeared by the dorms, did that mean she could teleport too?

She took a step, closing the distance between her and Simon. "Why do you want me here?"

"This is Demarcus Bartlett and Harry Wales. They're part of your group as well."

She pointed at Demarcus. "I've met Dreads before. We're from the same school."

"Excellent. Then we're a step ahead on team-building. The others are waiting for you all, so let's join them." Simon led them through a short corridor until they reached an even larger room with vaulted ceilings.

There, at a long wooden table, sat Lily and Sarah Jane.

Chapter Thirty-Five

Lily's heart leapt at the sight of her friends coming in. What were the odds that they'd all be in the same group? A Hispanic girl followed the boys in. She walked with a swagger and with searching eyes. Lily offered her a wave, and the girl nodded in return.

Simon motioned for everyone to sit down. The smooth wood gleamed in the light of the conference room. Harry made a beeline for Sarah Jane's side, so Demarcus joined Lily. The new girl hesitated, then she sat next to Demarcus. A soft leather chair enveloped her.

Now *this* was Silicon Valley.

"I'm glad everyone's here. Let me make the introductions." He pointed to each one in turn and gave their name and their hometown.

The girl was Rosa Gonzalez from San Jose. She kept eyeing the other teens and shifting around in her chair. Could she tell that the rest had become friends? Rosa's steely brown eyes focused on Simon. It might be awkward to have a new person affecting their group dynamics. Still, somehow luck had it that they all ended up together.

Simon laced his fingers together at the head of the table, his face a mask of concentration. A rush of confidence welled up within Lily, along with a feeling of trust. Today was going to be amazing. She truly had something to offer, like Simon had said. Despite her suffering and loss, she could do some remarkable things. With the guidance of Alturas, she would be a light to the world.

The lines on Simon's face relaxed and his easy smile returned. "You five made it through the screening. We knew there was some amazing potential here in central California, and after a long time of sifting through school records, test scores, interviews, and the results we gathered at the conference here, it's down to you."

He gestured to their group.

"Everyone we brought here to Launch has something to give. Each of you has something unique, special, and powerful to offer. It's time to realize your latent abilities."

Lily wondered where this was going. Yeah, her friends were here, but they were brand new friends. Could she fully trust them?

A familiar warmth filled her again. It would be all right.

Sarah Jane raised her hand. "Uh, Mr. Mazor? I wonder if you've made a mistake. With me, at least. There's nothing special about me. Very ordinary, right here."

Simon waved his hand over a small screen built into the end of the table. A holographic projection displayed in front of him, and he tapped some sort of virtual keyboard or interface. Lily couldn't help gasping at the sight. Everyone's eyes goggled at the fancy sci-fi tech.

Now a new projection extended from a camera in the ceiling. An outline of each of them slowly circled in the air above the table.

Simon stood and sauntered around the table. "You all are modest and inhibited. Maybe also deceived. And that is such a shame. This group right here may be the most impressive collection of teenagers the planet has ever seen."

The teens eyed each other. Lily knew something incredible was happening with her, but what was going on with everyone else? Were her friends keeping secrets as well?

"Sarah Jane, that includes you. We didn't make mistakes with this group. We take this too seriously. Tell me, when you dream, what do you dream about?"

Sarah Jane hesitated at first. Simon fixed his gaze on her. She sat up straighter and set her jaw. "I always dream about healing people. Or animals. Lately it's been every night. I'm always helping people with their injuries. But I've never thought of doing medicine. I hate needles."

"Believe or not, we picked up on that. My question is this: why are you dreaming about this so often? Isn't the subconscious a strong predictor of things to come for us?" Simon pulled a small metallic object out of his pocket. He flicked his wrist, and a blade clicked out. He walked over to Sarah Jane and knelt beside her.

"I believe in you." With those words he dragged the blade down his wrist, and blood squirted from the cleaved edges.

Everyone at the table screamed as red stained the carpet under Simon. Sarah Jane was near hysterical. "What on earth are you doing? Are you crazy?"

Simon winced but held his bleeding arm out in front of her. "No, I'm not crazy. I want you to embrace your potential. Heal me."

The frightened girl shook in her chair. Lily wanted to comfort her, except she felt paralyzed herself. Was this real? Or was Simon a madman?

"I ... I can't. I'm sorry."

"Then I'm going to be in a lot of trouble in a few minutes." Simon's face blanched as he took the blade and lined it up against his other wrist, blood running down his arm. "Can you at least try?"

A sob escaped her lips. "What do I do?"

Simon set the knife on one knee and took her hand in his. "Just believe. Focus on stopping the blood flow. Bring the skin together. I have faith."

Sarah Jane turned her head away, but set her hand on his. Her eyes squeezed shut as a squeal slipped out. A coppery scent drifted through the room. Lily's feet froze to the ground, but she whispered to her friend. "You can do this."

Her face scrunched up in concentration. She took Simon's lacerated wrist with both of hers and leaned over, pushing a grunt from her lungs. Then Sarah Jane jerked back with a gasp.

Simon twitched as well, then held up his arm for all to see.

Chapter Thirty-Six

The skin had stitched itself together—intact, all the blood gone.

Lily stared in disbelief. Simon had just slit his own wrist, and Sarah Jane had apparently healed it. The girl went pale, and her eyes started rolling back in her head. Lily found the strength to move her feet, and she dashed around the edge of the table to catch her. Then a rush of air passed her, and Demarcus caught Sarah Jane before she hit the floor.

He was behind Lily just a moment ago.

Rosa let out a low whistle. "Okay, then. Freckles here can heal, and Dreads can flat-out move."

Simon beamed as he knelt in front of Sarah Jane and waved some smelling salts under her nose. She shook her head and her eyes fluttered open. "You see? You're all special. Yes, Demarcus has super speed. Am I right?"

What could Demarcus say? They'd just caught him red-handed.

Demarcus's eyes expanded. "Uh, I think maybe it was just the adrenaline?"

Simon shook his head. "C'mon, man. Be real. You and I met earlier this weekend, don't you remember? I do, and I have the security footage that shows you at a thirty-mile-per-hour clip leaving the lunch room and running me over. I think I still have the mark."

Demarcus dropped his eyes. "I'm sorry about running you over. And yeah, I've got a gift with speed."

This was insane. They all had something special?

Sarah Jane shook her hands and backed against the wall. "My hands are hot now. I-I can't believe that just happened." Her voice trembled and her breath came out in ragged gasps.

Lily joined her roommate against the wall and whispered in her ear. "Shh, it's okay. Take some deep breaths. That was amazing!"

Simon spread his hands out wide with a smile that exuded excitement. "You guys are so freaking awesome! Do you even understand the impact of this? There's so much to accomplish if we all work together."

The group looked around at each other in silence.

"So, what can everyone else do?" Sarah Jane asked meekly.

Everyone else was thinking that too, Lily guessed. She swallowed, but the lump in her throat didn't want to dislodge. At the thought of revealing her abilities, her stomach flipped.

Simon took a couple of steps back and wagged his finger at them. "Hold that thought. It's time to go downstairs, gang."

He tapped something on his watch, and a hatch opened up behind them. The door pulled up, revealing a staircase descending into the floor. How many tricks did Alturas have in its buildings?

The stairs opened up into a wide room that defied description.

Lily turned in a circle as she took the sight in. Half gymnasium. Half future-tech-training-room-disco? She couldn't decide how to classify it. Wait—no disco ball, so it ruled that out. The rest seemed to fit.

Simon walked into the center, his arms held high and a broad smile brightening his face. "This, my new friends, is my Future Room. This is where we come to test out the newest toys from Alturas. I insist on being hands on with any products we make."

"Whoa. This is incredible. Err, what is it?" Harry asked.

The group filtered into the middle of the room. Mirrors lined one of the shorter walls. A large barbell set and rack of exercise equipment filled a corner opposite the mirrors. In another corner there was a smaller enclosed area, a curtain pulled back from the entrance, and a rubbery floor. Two alcoves built into the long walls contained a variety of gizmos and computer screens.

Simon clicked a button on his phone and an array of lights flashed all along the ceiling and walls. "This is designed for research and testing. All of these lights are sensors measuring everything from velocity, temperature, friction, speed—most any variable you can think of. If we can use things in a free atmosphere, we eliminate false readings or artificial usage when getting a data point."

Demarcus let out a low whistle. "This is crazy. Look at all this tech." He walked over to examine the exercise equipment closer.

Rosa flipped out her phone. "Yeah, this is cool. So why are we here? And why can't I get a signal?"

Simon walked over and put his hand over her phone. "We obviously can't let others see what we're doing here, so there's a signal dampener. And if someone were try to take a picture, all of the built-in cameras and lights would go off, ruining their exposure. If you don't mind, I'll ask you not pull out any personal electronic devices."

Rosa frowned, but slipped her phone in the back pocket of her shorts.

"As for your other question, what are you capable of? That's what we want to find out. Let's get some tests going to see what you can do."

Two Alturas staffers entered the room, smiles broad on their faces. "Gang, this is Kelsey, my assistant." He pointed to the woman with brown curly hair, dressed in skinny jeans, heels and a loose lavender blouse.

"And this is Jackson, my analyst." The man with blonde hair, a beard, and thick-framed glasses waved to them.

Simon clapped his hands. "Let's get this rolling. We've got a lot to accomplish this weekend."

Soon Lily, Rosa, and Demarcus were split up among different equipment. Lily shook her head in disbelief as she watched the proceedings. Demarcus had a VR visor on and ran on something Simon called a "dynamic treadmill" that was built into the floor. It allowed him to run, yet move side to side and continue moving.

Rosa had laughed at the weight that mechanical arms put on the dumbbells over at the exercise station. Jackson insisted that they increase the weight incrementally, yet each lift Rosa managed without any hint of strain. What was her limit?

As she watched the others work on their testing, Simon approached with hands behind his back. "Here's your equipment. It will allow you to let loose, but keep everyone else safe." He pulled his hands around to reveal a pair of metallic gauntlets, bulky things with wires protruding from the sides.

"What do I do with these?"

"You give us everything you've got." Simon's touch sent a thrill down her spine as he helped her into the ugly gauntlets. Lily tried to keep from blushing, but when she heard Rosa cough the name "Rudolph," she knew it wasn't working.

She held up her hands, encased in two torture devices. "Now what?"

"I've got your own VR feed to give you." He slipped an oversized pair of sunglasses on. His face was so close. A sweet, fruity scent wafted from his breath. Thoughts careened around her head from the sensory overload.

"This is an older prototype of a visual interface we hope to launch next year. This will work for our purposes today. They're synced to the gauntlets, so whatever you do, you'll see just in the glasses. No one has to suffer burned retinas." He winked at her.

A sigh sounded behind her. Lily turned to see Sarah Jane and Harry half-heartedly talking to each other. Harry especially looked downcast; his posture drooped. "What are they going to do?" Lily asked.

Simon glanced back. "We'll have a harder time testing their abilities. But I'm sure they're going to be vital going forward."

"What does Harry do? We already know about Sarah Jane healing you."

His finger touched his lips. "I'm not quite sure. He's got amazing readings. Our analysis hasn't quite defined his talent yet. Like you, I think he's just manifesting. Okay, are you ready?"

She offered her biggest smile. "Anytime." The gauntlets weighed down on her hands. She couldn't wait to get them off.

Simon patted her shoulder. "And here we go."

Chapter Thirty-Seven

Lily twitched when she pushed a strand of light forward with her mind and it happened in her visor. It would have shot Demarcus in the back if her hands were free. That was weird.

Simon pointed a small stylus at her glasses. "I'm triggering a program. See if you can hit the balls that will fall in your vision. Consider it a warm-up."

The gauntlets pinched her skin as she tried to blast the bouncing balls. Did she look like a total spaz? She missed the first several balls. The gauntlets threw off her timing, and they seemed to dampen her ability as well. Controlling light didn't come as easy with them. Finally, she figured out the delay and started hitting some.

"Good. Now give me your brightest light. What can you do there?" Simon tapped on his tablet, looking over results.

Time to shine. Lily closed her eyes and cleared her mind. She thought of how effortless it was to manipulate light in the Focuser. *I need to show Simon all I can do. Imagine it, then do it.* She pushed her hands out, giving it all she had.

A trickle of sweat broke out where she wore the glasses. Lily forced with all her might. The gauntlets heated up, letting her know that it was working.

Fatigue snuck up on her and the output waned. She relaxed and the gauntlets cooled right off. She wanted to wipe her brow, but the gauntlets made that impossible.

Simon looked over the readings on his tablet. "Not … bad. For a start they're pretty good. I bet you can do more, right?"

Her stomach dropped. That wasn't enough? Lily shook her hands as best she could to alleviate the tingling from pushing her power. She fought the urge to pout. *He wants more? I'll have to do better.*

A touch of anger flared inside her, and she thrust her hands out to blast an imaginary target, hoping that would help her crank things up. Just as she let the beam loose, Harry tumbled toward her.

Lily dove forward, but he cut her legs out from under her. Her torso landed with a heavy thud, knocking the wind out of her. The impact knocked her gauntlets loose, and her beam of energy blew them off and struck Rosa straight in the chest. Rosa flew backwards with a grunt. The barbells she had been holding thundered on the floor with its impact.

What just happened? Lily rolled onto her back, trying to catch her breath. Beside her, loud groaning came from Harry. Before she could even sit up, Rosa stood above her.

"¡Qué susto! What was that?" She reached down and picked Lily up with one hand. Lily dangled from her shirt as Rosa scowled at her.

Simon scrambled to get a hand on Rosa. "It's okay. Lily didn't mean to do that. She was knocked over by Harry."

All of the anger seemed to melt out of Rosa's face. She set Lily down and took a step back. Lily made sure her tank top covered everything while sucking in air.

"Sorry about that. I have a temper, and didn't know what had happened," Rosa explained.

"It's okay. I'm sorry I blasted you. Are you okay?"

Simon kept a hand on Rosa as she answered. "Yeah, I'm good. Part of my gift is that I can take a lot of punishment. It takes a lot to hurt me."

Lily wished it were the same for her. Her chest ached and her hands hurt from the gauntlets being jarred off. Her head throbbed and little lights sparkled in her peripheral vision. She shook her head, but she still had some visual changes. An aura of black hung around Rosa's head. Weird.

Another moan sounded behind her. Demarcus tried to help Harry up, who favored his right leg in the process. He tried to put weight on it, but he almost buckled, and Demarcus had to steady him.

Everyone gathered around. "What happened?" Simon asked, a hard glint in his eyes. That seemed unusual for him, Lily thought.

"Oh man, that kills. I—I leaned in to see what Demarcus was doing, and stepped too far. He moved so fast my foot yanked out from under me and then I bowled Lily over. Did I hurt you?"

The visual changes had faded, and only minor aches remained. "Don't worry. Hey, what's up with your knee?"

"I don't know. I can't even stand on it."

A sound of a throat clearing brought their attention to Sarah Jane, standing behind everyone. "Maybe I have a way to practice after all. Do you mind if I try my ability?"

Harry's eyes lit up like beacons, with a silly grin to accompany them. "I wouldn't mind at all." Lily smiled at the thought of Harry and Sarah Jane together.

The Alturas staffers leaned in close. They hadn't seen Sarah Jane's magic yet. Lily managed to stay near Simon. Thankfully Rosa returned to the exercise equipment. A very large punching bag hung from a thick rod that protruded from the wall. Rosa started throwing blows that echoed throughout the room.

Sarah Jane knelt down next to Harry and cupped his injured knee gently. He winced at the action. Holy crap, his knee had swollen just since he first stood up. She closed her eyes in concentration.

Harry's eyes rolled back for a moment. Was he going to pass out? No, they snapped straight and he let out a low whistle. "Oh man, that is wild."

Sarah Jane's hand flew to her chest. "Did I hurt you?"

"No. That feels great!" He put his foot down and let go of Demarcus. He jogged around with a whoop.

Lily couldn't keep from grinning. What would they accomplish with Simon mentoring them?

Simon didn't celebrate. He frowned as he read a message on his phone. His brows crunched together and he grit his teeth before putting the device away and putting his host face back on.

"Great job, Sarah Jane. I knew you could do it. Unfortunately, something critical has come up that I have to run and take care of. I'll leave you guys here with Kelsey and Jackson until noon. We'll all meet at the front of the building at one o'clock and we'll dive in deeper." He gave a quick wave as he climbed the stairs.

Lily stretched her arms out to keep loose. Rosa's blows on the punching bag punctuated the quiet as Kelsey and Jackson took readings on Harry's knee. A cough alerted Lily to Demarcus standing behind.

"Did you see how much Rosa lifted?" He pointed to the weight set.

"Nope. Was it a lot?"

"The last I saw she benched 400 pounds. Benched! That's a huge amount for deadlifting, much less not using her legs. And she didn't seem to struggle at all."

Lily noticed that Demarcus had pretty good definition in his arms. "How much can you bench?"

"At my best I've done 180 pounds. That was after a semester of weightlifting. And how tall is she? Like five-foot-two? That's just insane."

Great. Rosa said everything was okay from their accident, but she acted cool ever since it happened.

"The takeaway is: don't mess with her?" Lily whispered.

"Probably."

Chapter Thirty-Eight

Demarcus wanted another spin on the dynamic treadmill. The VR headset made it seem like he was in a real-life video game. He dodged cars and obstacles with his body really moving, while the treadmill kept him in one spot. Such an amazing experience, until Harry got too close. The momentum Demarcus created sent Harry flying.

Jackson ran a scanner over Harry, who held his arms out and looked uncomfortable with all the attention. "I still can't get a reading on what your gift is. You've got high metrics, but nothing specific."

Could someone's face get any redder? Harry shook his head. "I don't really know what to tell you. You guys must have made a mistake."

A beep went off on Jackson's watch. He tapped the side of his glasses and read the display. "Lunch is in ten minutes. Kelsey, don't we need to show them something else before then?"

Kelsey nodded while gesturing to bring everyone in. "C'mon with me, gang. You're going to love this."

Demarcus led the way up the stairs behind Kelsey. This was way too much of a trip. He wasn't alone in having a gift. Five of them lived in central California alone! What was going on in the world? Radiation from that Japanese nuclear plant meltdown? Genetically modified foods? Some secret government testing program gone horribly awry?

And to think that Lily and Sarah Jane had such talents. There was no way this was all a coincidence. The four of them becoming friends and being initiated into the target group for the conference? He didn't know about Rosa though. She didn't seem inclined to play nice with others, even though she had apologized to Lily.

One question nagged at Demarcus, so he gave in. "Rosa, the first night I thought I recognized you and followed you around the dorms. When I was distracted for a moment you disappeared. How'd you do that if you've got super strength?"

A slight blush colored her cheeks. "There was a cute guy up on the third floor I wanted to talk to. They wouldn't let me in the boys' hallway at that time of night, so I jumped to the balcony and slipped in. My legs are pretty strong too." She winked.

"You knew before coming here?"

"Maybe. What about you? I seem to recall you being in a walking boot or something earlier this year."

"That's when I noticed something different. When my doctor released me from treatment and I started testing it out, I started running faster and faster. I can outrun cars on the freeway now."

Lily whistled. "Wow. Good thing no one caught you before this, or they'd haul you off to be studied."

The headache that had been plaguing him for the last hour had finally subsided. A figure flashed in his mind. Lily's comment had triggered a faint memory.

John. He'd said these were gifts given for such a time as this. Even though the other ideas appealed to his geeky side, he felt a reassurance that God had His hand in all of this. He couldn't wait to tell John about the girls.

They made a couple of turns and found another staircase to the second story where they found a full locker room with men's and women's facilities. Kelsey stopped before the doors and waited for everyone to gather.

"My apologies that Simon had to take care of some urgent business. He is very much looking forward to working with you all. Inside the locker rooms you'll find a locker with your name on it. There are some items for you in there. Everyone at the conference will get a jacket similar to yours in appearance. Yours, however, are designed with microfibers to protect you from moderate injuries. Alturas wants to protect their investment in you. You can go check them out now."

Demarcus and Harry ducked into the men's side. Sure enough, two lockers in the middle had their names on them. White jackets with red trim, to match Flare's color scheme, hung inside. They looked and felt like training gear, slightly thicker than the typical sportswear Demarcus had worn in the past. The lightweight jackets fit them both well, and they took a moment to admire the style on each other. Now Demarcus felt like he was part of the company.

He slipped the jacket off since it was in the eighties outside. Still, how awesome to get swag like this?

Demarcus's phone vibrated in his pocket. They had a moment, so he pulled it out. It was a text message from John: "Meet me at the hamburger restaurant across from the campus at lunch. Bring your friends. I will purchase your meals."

Awfully formal for a text message, but it would be good for them to hear from John. He had some definite insight. Demarcus wondered how he'd view Simon's preaching about potential.

The time on his phone said 11:30. They'd break for lunch soon anyway. "Harry, John wants us to meet with him at In-N-Out Burger for lunch and to bring the girls. He said he needed to talk to all of us."

"Do you think they'll mind if we leave? I mean, after dinner was our free time the other night."

"Nah, it'll be fine. We're next door. Plus, he's buying."

They stepped out of the locker room and waited for the girls.

When they finally came out, all three of them chattered excitedly. Even Rosa was joining in. They each wore similar jackets to Demarcus's and Harry's, except it seemed like the jackets were specifically tailored for each of them. The feminine cut of their gear made them look like athletes.

Kelsey stepped forward as she looked at her tablet. "You can leave your jackets here since it's so hot. Simon wants to start working with you at 1:00 P.M., okay?"

She led them back down to the main room.

As they hit the door, Demarcus motioned them to the side. "Hey gang, instead of the cafeteria, let's hit the In-N-Out Burger across from the parking lot. Harry and I have a friend, an elderly guy, who wants to buy us lunch."

Rosa crossed her arms. "Why do you want to have lunch with an old dude?"

"The thing is, he knows about our powers. He said that we have them for a reason. You need to hear it from him."

Harry chimed in. "He's cool. I thought he was a little crazy at first, but we should see what he has to say."

"How does he know about our gifts?" Rosa asked.

Demarcus and Harry shared a look. "He saw me use my speed to help Harry the other night—" A slight elbow from Harry ended the story before he explained the set up to that incident.

"You're saying he saw you and that's how he knows."

Words escaped him. "Well, he seemed to know things about them besides that."

Rosa shook her head. "No thanks. I'll catch you guys later. I've got a couple of people to catch up with myself." She sat down on the steps and pulled out her phone, her thumbs flying across the screen.

Lily and Sara Jane shared a look.

"Yeah, we'll go," Sarah Jane replied. "Someone else that knows about our gifts? That's interesting, and what will it hurt?"

They took off down the sidewalk. Demarcus slipped on his Oakleys and peeked to see if Rosa was heading this way since the cafeteria was in the same direction. Instead, she'd disappeared.

Oh, well. Her loss. He shrugged and took the lead toward burger heaven.

Chapter Thirty-Nine

Simon came out of the lift from the basement testing room to his office on the main floor. Otto stood with two security guards who both looked nervous. Simon sat down in his plush work chair and pulled up a couple of holographic screens from his glass-topped desk.

"What's the status?"

Otto cleared his throat. "IT found an anomaly when doing today's security clearance scan. Somehow a custodian got Level-A clearance and entered the main labs to clean. He made it into the sensory lab. He stopped and read a few papers. The guards responded and found him talking with a couple of the conference guests. They took his badge and relieved him of his of duties."

Simon played the video on the computer screen while he prepared to pull up demographic information on the holographic display. "What's his name?"

Otto glanced at his display. "John Presbus. He's been working here for two months. Excellent reviews by his supervisors. Diligent and does quality work."

The video showed the custodian moving past blueprints for the Source down to some discarded food items. He cleaned thoroughly, but Simon picked up on a discrepancy.

"That's wonderful. We have a diligent corporate thief. Did you see this?" He flicked the feed from his monitor to the holographic desktop, which played it out in 3D. "After this John left, where did the Nullifiers go?"

Otto pointed to the counter. "He put it right there. Except, it's not there. How did he do that?"

Simon slapped a folder off the desk, papers fluttering to the ground. "Sleight of hand! And then you fired him and let him go? Did you search him?"

The guards looked down, avoiding eye contact. Simon focused his gaze on them, concentrating.

The shorter one looked up with a glassy sheen over his eyes. "We checked him and there wasn't anything on him. After he left, Elias couldn't find his Eraser."

Elias shared the same vacant stare. "I don't know what happened to it."

Simon relaxed, rubbing his temple. The two idiots were telling the truth. So, somehow, this geezer had managed to nab two of their secret, experimental tools. Brilliant. Where was this John?

"You two are dismissed. Report to HR for further instructions."

The shamed guards left, and Otto stood in front of him, wringing the paper in his hands. "What do you want us to tell HR?"

"Oh, they're fired. This John—we need to find him. Get his records, find his address, see if we can hack his phone, and scour his networks. If he's trying to sell secrets to one of our competitors, he's going to be sorry."

A knock sounded on the door. Who would that be?

He flicked his hand over a control and the door opened. The strong girl stood before them. Rosa. He could feel the submission radiating from her. She was so broken, so hungry for something to make her feel whole.

"Hey. Thought you might want to know that your other pets left the campus. Said they're meeting with some old dude who claims he knows about our abilities too."

Simon growled. The situation had just deteriorated.

Chapter Forty

L ily scampered after the boys, dragging Sarah Jane behind her. Her sandals slapped against the pavement in their rush. The walk light had stopped, and the right-turn traffic waited for them to finish crossing. Leave it to guys to bolt across when there was hardly any time left.

A very old-looking man stood by the door to the restaurant, his eyes constantly scanning the Alturas campus. He opened the door for them. "Please, get whatever you want, and we'll eat outside. We need to talk."

They ordered their favorites and met him at the picnic table after he paid. They all thanked him for the generosity. Lily lifted the bun and smelled the grilled onions. Perfect.

Demarcus introduced the girls. "There's another gal, Rosa, who wouldn't come. She's got super strength."

John's withered hand stroked the white whiskers on his chin. "Hmm. A Samson-type. We will need to find a way to reach her." He focused on Lily and Sarah Jane. "Oh, excuse me. I am John, and I am pleased to meet you all. Shalom. Grace and peace to you."

Lily returned his handshake. A gentle, firm grip. A ripple of peace flowed through her. She didn't think she'd been wound up, but something relaxed her.

Harry looked worried. "What happened when the security guys took you away?"

Demarcus looked up from his bacon cheeseburger. A dab of mustard lingered on his chin. "What are you talking about, dude?"

Security had to haul this guy away? John seemed harmless enough. He had drawn-in cheeks, bushy eyebrows, and a lot of laugh lines along his light brown eyes. The color almost looked as if it had faded over the years. Something about those eyes suggested they'd seen a lot in their time.

"I fear you won't remember, Demarcus. Before you went to The Cove, the security guards removed me and revoked my badge. Apparently, I got caught on-camera being somewhere I was not supposed to be. Even though my card let me in. They could not explain that one. It must have been some sort of providence. Anyway, they pointed a mind wipe device at you, and it must have deleted a small portion of your memory. At least, that is what the instructions indicate."

"Wait. You know what they supposedly zapped me with?"

John slipped a small black device with a matte finish out of his khaki pants. "It was this. The guard neglected to care for it as they took me to HR."

Sarah Jane sat with saucer eyes taking it all in. Lily couldn't decide what to think of John. Was he senile? Or just deluded? Her temperature rose. At least, her Alturas band felt warm to the touch.

Lily cleared her throat. "I'm sorry—Alturas kicked you out because you were snooping and then stole from them?" She flicked a strand of hair away from her food. "Shouldn't any company do that?"

"All is not as it seems, but I understand your confusion. Now, you are the girl of light, correct?"

Lily raised an eyebrow. "How did you know?"

"That was an impressive light show you put on last night. Very lovely."

John turned to regard Sarah Jane. "And how about you, dear? What is your gift?"

She sat in silence for a moment. On the way over she'd confessed to Lily that she had prayed for a hurt dog before, and it ran off without a limp afterward. Otherwise she'd had no idea until Simon did the stunt with the knife. "I guess I can heal."

He clasped his hands together. "Wonderful! Such a special gift. It comes with a burden, though. You must be very compassionate, and that makes it hard if you can't help everyone you want."

Sarah Jane gaped at him.

Lily waved a fry in the air. "How do you know about this?"

"It was prophesied long ago that in a time of growing darkness, gifts would be given to a group of people to stand against it. I have been waiting for this a very long time. The rise of the anointed."

Demarcus scratched his head. "I still can't remember being zapped."

Harry elbowed him. "That's the point, yeah? You wanted to talk to us, John? It sounded urgent."

"Yes. Alturas set up this conference to screen for people with special abilities. There's something going on with mind control and trying to broadcast it out into the world to influence young people."

The sound of cars passing hovered in the background. Lily couldn't take another bite. What was this old coot talking about?

Demarcus cleared his throat, took a sip of Coke, and tried again. "Um, that sounds pretty wild, if you know what I mean. Why would this place be doing all that? I mean, Flare is becoming the biggest social network with teens and college students anyway. Why would they need to do that?"

John pointed a finger in the air. "Exactly. How did they grow popular so fast? And what better way to infiltrate culture and change things than by corrupting young people? If they have that ability, then the whole world will bend to their whim. And, with what I've read, I do not think you are alone in having gifts. I believe Mr. Mazor has a special ability as well. That is how he knew how to look for you, how to find you."

Lily shook her head. She'd heard enough. "Did you lose your tin-foil hat?"

He squinted at her. "What do you mean?"

"You know, to protect you from the brain waves they're sending out to influence you. Works in all the conspiracy theory movies. Maybe we can ask the girl at the counter if they have foil for to-go orders. We can fashion some out of that if you don't mind some ketchup. It might just work."

John shook his head. "No, that won't do it. There's something else you need instead—"

Lily stood up. She couldn't take this anymore, even if he was some kind of friend to her buddies. "Look, Simon is an amazing man. He's brought us here and helped us unlock our potential already. I didn't know I could manipulate light; Sarah Jane didn't realize she could heal. But we've got these amazing talents, and he's going to help us explore these gifts and use them to impact the world. All he's done is be generous and accepting of us."

She pointed to Demarcus. "You kept wondering what brought us all together. I think I figured it out. We're all broken. Every one of the attendees—we're a mess. Yet Simon is helping us become more than we ever thought possible. I'm sorry guys, but I'm not going to sit here and listen to any more of these wild accusations."

Lily didn't expect tears, but drops of salt water trickled down her cheeks, the taste hitting her lips. "See you later."

Sarah Jane stood up and chased after her. "Lily, wait up."

Lily skirted the fence for the eating area and caught the traffic light just in time to sprint back to Alturas with her roommate trailing behind her.

Chapter Forty-One

Demarcus sat with a lead weight in his gut. The half-eaten burger didn't look appealing at all. Here he'd been listening to an old man he'd barely met, trusting what he had to say. Now he sounded like a crackpot. Lily was right. What were they thinking?

A whisper filtered into his ear. He looked up to find John's lips moving with an occasional sound slipping out, something that sounded like a foreign language. Harry held his head with his elbows leaning on the table. So much for lunch.

Well, if John was going to start talking to himself, they might as well go. He nodded his head toward the campus. "Dude, let's go."

Harry caught Demarcus's arm and held him, his grip surprisingly strong. "No. Don't you see what John's doing? He's praying. You're the one who told me he had a connection to God. Well, I believe him. All of it. There's something not right here.

"Why did those guards drag him off? Why did they zap you, and suddenly you can't remember the last thing that just happened? I didn't know what to say in that gym, but I didn't want to let Simon know what I could do. I have a bad feeling about this."

Demarcus lowered himself back onto the bench. What should he do? Yes, Lily made sense when she'd called all of this crazy. Still, every time John came around, Demarcus sensed peace. What fit with what he learned from his mom, the Bible, and what God had for people?

If nothing else, he needed to pray about it on his own. John's silent supplication continued in the background. Demarcus bowed his head and asked for wisdom.

Lord, what do we do? We need your light to guide us.

Pictures rushed through his mind. Sitting in the interview room, answering crazy questions. The Focuser, picking out his deep subconscious. The strange way he felt when Simon appeared on stage. The man had such a draw. It was almost like he pulled everyone to him.

Then three fuzzy figures separated in his brain. The focus cleared, and he remembered John being pulled away by the guards. The scene rewound in his head. The guards backed off. John had slipped something into his hands before they got there.

Demarcus lifted his head. "John, what did you give me earlier?" He fished down into his pocket and pulled out the two containers, the little gadget with a small light on the tip, and the screen.

John raised his arms in the sky. "Hallelujah! I did not know if you still had them or not. Let me see the sensor."

Demarcus handed it over, but John grabbed his wrist.

"What do you have on?"

"They gave us these bracelets at the start of the conference. They're supposed to provide a constant Wi-Fi hotspot for us."

John aimed the sensor at the band and squeezed the small trigger on the side. The bars on the screen immediately filled up.

"Full-strength. Watch this." He stood up and took a few steps away and pointed it to the sky. "No bars."

Harry straightened. "What does that mean?"

"I found this and used it around the campus. There are hot spots and areas with poor reception depending on the buildings and their orientation to the source. Those router boxes in each building always recorded higher, showing they amplified the signal."

Demarcus checked his band. It seemed fine. "Okay, so we get a good Wi-Fi signal."

"No. Do you not see? This is the signal that comes from Alturas that affects people. It is not just for your phone or a computer. It is intended to control you."

Lily crossed the campus, fighting back tears. How could Demarcus and Harry listen to that crackpot attack Simon? After all he'd done for them, the fact that no one else defended him disappointed her. Sarah Jane trailed along, not saying anything.

They passed the cafeteria in silence. Her frustration grew with every step. She could almost feel it as a tingle throughout her skin.

Sarah Jane scurried up beside her and held her hand. "Hey, are you okay?"

Lily sighed. "How can they just let that crazy old guy trash Simon like that? I don't know what to think." She waved her hands in twirling circles as she spoke.

Sarah Jane pulled her close to speak in her ear. "I know you're upset, but you need to calm down. Either that or figure out how to control your power. You're putting on a light show."

She looked down. Threads of light streamed from her fingertips. Whoa. She peeked over her shoulder. No one seemed to notice that a girl was glowing. Thankfully it was midday, and the sun muted the effect. "Thanks. I didn't know it could go off like that." She inhaled a few deep, calming breaths, and the illumination faded.

"It's okay. John is only one man with an opinion. I'm sure Simon has enemies. You don't get to a position like his without having people come against you. What harm can this one guy do?"

"I don't want him influencing our friends. What do you think he's telling them?"

Sarah Jane gave her a quick squeeze. "If they're our friends, then it'll be okay. We'll work through it. I trust them, just like I trust you. Just relax. They'll see the light," she said with a wink. "C'mon, let's go over to Simon's headquarters. We'll be there a little early. I'm sure that'll be fine."

Lily looked back to the burger place in the distance. "Do you think we should tell Simon about this John?"

"Wait a second. They're *controlling* us? These signals across the campus are mind-control waves?" It sounded like being in a science fiction movie. The idea almost sounded cool, except it was really happening. Demarcus rubbed his wrist where the band had been. "How do you know?"

"The documents you found described what was happening. I had to piece things together, and I did some more digging. It seems Simon wields some kind of influence ability. Like super-charisma. It does not seem to fully be mind-control, but it aligns people with him. And I think he wants to use you and your friends for spreading this. This conference, what is it about?"

Harry finished off his fries. At least he had an appetite. "It's using our potential to influence our peers and the world."

"Does it say anywhere that they intend to influence people for good?"

Both Demarcus and Harry went to speak and paused.

"Honestly, no. I can't think that they said that," Harry finally said.

John inhaled deeply. "I was called here to investigate this and to gather the anointed. So far things are not going very well. Still, we need to do what we can. I worry that the girls may find themselves in a very tight spot."

"Why do you say that?" Demarcus couldn't get his mind around everything.

"I failed to find anything concrete, but the conference dates were critical, mentioned in all of the things I read. They were targeting this weekend specifically, with the culmination being something called a 'transference.' The summer solstice tomorrow is their target. I think they want to use all of the attendees, yet it seems that you five were specially chosen.

"And Lily identified the connecting factor with everyone, I believe. Everyone here has been broken in some way. I think it makes people more susceptible to Simon's power."

Harry put his palms on the table. "So, you're saying we could be in danger? The girls? What about Sarah Jane?"

Wait a minute. Did Harry have a thing for Sarah Jane? He was acting all smooth with Lily earlier.

John fixed his gaze on them. "I do not know what purpose it would serve for Simon to hurt them. You need to understand that this is more than a battle of wits or of the physical. It is foremost a spiritual battle. If Simon is using this gift for control then ultimately the inspiration to do that comes from the Enemy.

"The forces of darkness seek to steal people away from the Light of the gospel, and I know that lies at the heart of this battle. And if Satan is involved, it can be deadly. The demonic will not hesitate to hurt whoever gets in the way."

The bottom fell out of Demarcus's stomach. Could that really happen? Could such a positive experience take such a dark turn?

"What can we do?" Demarcus asked.

John walked over to the boys and put his hands on their shoulders. "First of all, do not fear. The Lord is with us. I think the next step is for you both to go back and be my eyes and ears. Obviously, I cannot without my badge and clearance. I will stay nearby if you need me, but I had better not be found there without an important reason. You have my phone number."

Harry tapped his band. "We should probably take these off so Simon can't get to us. What if we return to the campus without them? Will he know?"

The elder tossed one of the plastic cases to each of them. "These are Nullifiers. They are designed to protect against his power, I believe. They are little stickers with a tiny circuit built in. Just act like Simon still has sway over you, and he probably will not know the difference."

Demarcus pulled the miniature band-aid out. A tiny diagram showed the sticker placed behind the ear. Good, his dreads would hide it. Harry's close-cropped hair around his neckline would make his more prominent, though.

Once he affixed the Nullifier, a quick attack of double vision hit, then faded. Huh. Something had been affecting him after all.

"Did you feel a change when you put your patch on? It felt like my eyes crossed just now." Harry squeezed his eyes shut for a moment.

"Yeah, I did. John, do you have any more? If our heads just cleared, that means Lily and Sarah Jane are being impacted by Simon's suggestions as well."

"Unfortunately, I do not. You should return to the campus, though, so as not to appear suspicious. I will be praying for you and ready to come as fast as I can if needed. Be brave and strong, for the Lord goes with you. And He will watch over your friends as well."

Harry glanced over his shoulder towards the campus. "Sure. Two kids against a mind-control genius and his campus of brilliant staff. No problem."

Chapter Forty-Two

Simon flipped through the dossier on Lily Beausoliel while waiting for the signal from his Master. All pertinent information needed to be at the ready when talking with him.

First, the analysis from the time in the Future Room confirmed that she could power the Source. Her power levels amazed him. She would need help to unlock her full potential, and she had the chance to be someone truly special.

The background data painted a typical picture. Recently moved. Social problems at school. Those who were detached made likely prospects. She lived with her father and new stepmother in Palo Alto. Her mother and younger brother died in a car accident almost two years ago. An apt trigger for the brokenness required.

Wait. A strange notation in the margin of her report. It referenced another paper further in her folder. Simon flipped through the analysis papers until he reached a police report. Details of the accident. A pang hit his chest as he read through it. The mother had mixed her prescriptions, including too much pain medication, and it cost the family dearly.

No, that wasn't right. This was not the original report. Simon pulled up the electronic records and sifted through them until he found the same police file. With a few lines of code, he uncovered the true report.

It was no accident. Someone had done it on purpose. And unless the code in the file was another misdirection ploy, the digital finger pointed to the Archai.

A light next to the door in the corner blinked. Simon closed the electronic records and hurried to pull the heavy wooden door open. A blast from a tank shell couldn't penetrate the steel core of the door.

He entered the narrow chamber, his mind racing about Lily's case. Someone rigged her mother's accident and covered it up. To facilitate the triggering of her gift?

A green glow emanated in the chamber and a silhouetted figure flickered on the thin film of jade before him.

"What is the status of the project?" The Master's voice didn't waste time with pleasantries. His master had shown him how to use his gift to affect people, and he expected a full return on his investment.

"We identified five different teens with special abilities. All broken. Most importantly, we found the one with the optics control. She's very powerful, but she's just now discovering her latent potential. The fiber optic lines are all completed, so we were planning to execute Phase Three on the solstice, after I've worked with the girl today and tomorrow in maximizing her ability."

After three years of planning and preparation, the day to begin Phase Three had finally arrived. The secure network required to spread the message of the Archai now spanned the globe. With new insights into fiber optics and optimizing the function of this medium, they'd forge a path that no one could stop.

The last step: A specific kind of gifted who could use her power to propel Simon's own influence along the fiber optic cables and fuel the revolution along the whole network.

The Master's deep voice rumbled, "And what of the setbacks?"

How did he know? "We did have an employee steal a few items from us. Two Nullifiers and a signal tracer. He may have gotten an Eraser as well. And, apparently, he has been talking with four people in our target group. We don't know what he's been telling them or how it may affect things."

"Do you know who this man is?"

Simon picked up his tablet with the HR information. "His name is John Presbus. He has a long history of custodial work and has excellent references. Nothing suggested that he would participate in any corporate espionage or sabotage." He strategically omitted Rosa's comment that he may have known about the gifted teens.

"How old does it say he is?"

That seemed like an odd question. Simon wasn't about to second-guess the Master. "It says he's sixty-five years old. His picture looks like he could be older. Work reports from management show he's been an exemplary worker until today."

Simon beamed the tablet's information across the network for the Master to review.

A low growl escaped through the connection. "Do you know who this is? He is a legend long thought to be dead, yet he still lives. And now he is here to interfere with our plans. If my adversary sent him, it is serious."

Simon fiddled with his rolled-up sleeve. "How should we proceed, then?"

The shadow leaned forward. "Accelerate the timetable. We cannot give him time to interfere. Start the transference today. And do whatever you can to keep this John from getting involved."

"Will the transference work?"

A ghostly hand waved on the screen. "It will be enough. We cannot risk losing the opportunity if John marshals forces against us."

"Do you want him eliminated?" It was something Simon never thought he'd need to consider, but if the Master was this concerned, every option was on the table.

"Suffice it to say, it cannot be done. That is why you must act now. Get the girl, plug her in, and send out the signal. Once that happens, he will have failed and will be unable to stop the advancement."

Simon would've given his Alturas empire for a glass of water right now. His throat was so parched. "My concern is that I haven't been able to mentally prep the girl. She may not be able to handle the process."

"It must be done today. The signal will achieve full coverage with her abilities. If she does not survive, it is the cost of progress. You understand the consequences here, do you not?"

Simon swallowed, the constriction of his throat threatening to close off his airway. "I understand, sir. I will start the project now."

"No delays. And failure will not be tolerated."

PART
3

Chapter Forty-Three

The doors for Simon's headquarters swung open when Lily and Sarah Jane got there. A couple of guards held the doors open wide for them. Another effect of Demarcus's loony old man. All of a sudden, the campus had to be guarded.

Kelsey approached them as soon as they entered. "Simon will be with you in a few minutes."

The girls plopped onto the leather cushions. Lily let her fingers glide over the surface. She'd never felt such soft leather. She could sink into the comfort here.

Excitement pulsed through her with every heartbeat. She didn't have to keep her ability a secret anymore! She wouldn't show it off to just anyone, but she had a mentor in Simon. He would help her develop it and guide her.

Her old feelings of being worthless slipped away like an old snakeskin. No longer would she be defined as the girl with an addict for a mother—a woman who'd killed her son while driving high. Lily had something to offer. She was renewed, a new creature.

A text buzzed through on her phone. It was Demarcus. "Where R U?"

She hesitated. As her first contact at the conference, Demarcus had become special to her in just a couple of days. Still, she didn't want to deal with that foolish old guy. Ah, well, like Sarah Jane said, they could deal with each other and work it through.

She texted back, "At Simon's."

The reply came through. "On our way."

Good. Hopefully they wouldn't have issues with the boys, and they'd all work together in this group to make the kind of worldwide difference Simon kept talking about.

Rosa came in from the rear of the main sitting room. Had she not even left? Lily still didn't trust her. She was sick of the bullying from Missy. No way would she take it from another chick.

Rosa stopped in front of the couch with an intense glare in her eyes. "Simon needs us right now. There's something important he needs us to do."

Sarah Jane jumped up and started over to her. "Let's go, Lily. We want to see what's going on."

Before she got up, she glimpsed the last message from Demarcus. "Be smart."

Chapter Forty-Four

Simon climbed the stairs to the rooftop of his specially-built residence office. That he could enjoy such a palatial headquarters still amazed him.

The vision began with launching something that spoke to his generation and infusing it with his special touch. By working with some brilliant computer nerd friends, they had fused the connections of Facebook, the visual appearance of Pinterest, and the immediacy of Twitter into one interface: Flare.

He stepped out of the stairwell and onto the roof of the building. The air swirled by him, ruffling his hair as he walked over to the Source. The view from up here thrilled him each time he stepped out. The sprawling campus was just the beginning of what he could do. Flare was only the tool. Soon he would stand by his Master and bring the change that the world desperately needed.

All the work, the trouble, the pain—it would be worth it.

He focused on the Source. Strips of gold protected rare earth cables that crisscrossed along the surface of the sphere. Two hand plates mounted on the rear beckoned him to use them. Up front sat a chair with a headset and built-in gloves for the light-wielder to use.

The impulse from the girl would fire into the Source, reflect back and forth until it saturated the signal from Simon, and feed it into two massive cables that ran through the centers of the front columns of the building. From there, it would filter out to the worldwide network, allowing the limited reach of his influence to permeate every computer and each smartphone that ran Flare.

Right now, he could directly impact people within a room on his own. The router system on campus amplified the effect to a degree. The Source would change everything.

He felt the cool metal squares under his hands. It didn't feel right, to possibly sacrifice Lily for this. If he'd only had the full time of the conference. He was sure that his natural ability to bring out the best in people would enable her to give what was needed without it being stripped from her. She appeared to be a sweet, if wounded, girl. He hated the idea of strapping her in and flipping the switch.

Also, she'd do it with her own consent. Well, perhaps not fully, considering his influence. The snippet that the Archai had maneuvered things far before the Launch Conference concerning Lily's mother also pricked his subconscious. If they could play such a long game with one girl …

But the Master had left no quarter. Simon knew what had to be done.

As he felt the squares, heat surged from his hands into the gold and reverberated into the orb. Pumping his power into it wouldn't go far, but with all of the bracelets developed as mobile routers for his power, he could control the attendees and staff. It would set them up as defense for what was about to happen. He needed to establish precautions if anyone got any strange ideas from the mysterious old man snooping on their plans.

The orb started humming, a high-pitched whine that oscillated in volume. His mind control was reflecting, bouncing off the interior and concentrating to augment the signal. A drop of salty sweat dripped down his nose. He focused on the instructions for the staff and attendees, the mental suggestion to guide them for the next hour or so.

The Source vibrated with the intensity of the process. Simon pinpointed his suggestion to the single idea needed, knowing the potency would be hard to resist at that point.

Would the Source hold up to both his power and Lily's?

The hum turned into a loud, solid tone. It was ready. With one final mental push, he released his hands and raised them in the air. A wave of energy emitted from the Source, and a faint crimson trail hovered in its wake as it washed over the Alturas campus.

Using his power in such a concentrated manner invigorated him. Adrenaline pumped through his blood, charging his cells with renewed energy. Time to step into destiny.

He walked to the ledge and peered over. The attendees began pouring out of the classroom hall, heading toward his building. A makeshift army.

Chapter Forty-Five

Lily and Sarah Jane followed Rosa up the labyrinth of hallways and stairs to the top of the building. She held up her palm. "We need to wait here for Simon."

Sarah Jane was rubbing her wrist all the way up, and she took off the Alturas bracelet while they waited. A reddish rash with tiny blisters spread around her arm where the bracelet had been.

"What is that?" Lily couldn't believe the reaction on her friend's skin.

"I've got a metal allergy. Things like nickel cause something called a contact dermatitis. Kind of like eczema. Something in this bracelet must be triggering it." She gouged her skin with her nails. "Oh, it itches like crazy."

Rosa smirked. "Why don't you heal yourself?"

Lily took a step toward the snarky girl. "Look, what is your deal? We barely met you and you're on her case. I'm telling you, right now, back off."

She had a few inches on the diminutive Hispanic girl, but Rosa squared her shoulders and didn't stand down. "Let her stand up for herself if it's a problem. And what are you going to do, Nightlight?"

Lily balled her fists. Good thing her mind worked fast enough to realize she wouldn't beat this girl with strength. The demonstration with weights stood out. She had to use her power in such a way to neutralize Rosa's brawn.

"It doesn't seem to work."

Both Lily and Rosa looked to Sarah Jane. She wrapped her wrist with her other hand and pulled it off to reveal the same blemish. No change.

"So you can't even heal yourself?"

"Well, I've never tried before. Maybe it's something that only works on others."

Rosa laughed. "Let's test it again."

Her hands wrapped around Lily's bracelet and squeezed so hard that the metal cut into the forearm. Lily screamed as a popping sound came from her wrist. She staggered backwards holding her arm.

The bracelet crackled with an electrical charge, sending shocking pain into her lacerated skin and snapped bone. Lily's fingers clawed at the metal. It broke into pieces and clattered on the ground. The flesh around her wrist looked like fresh hamburger.

Lily's vision focused into a tunnel. A cry from Sarah Jane sounded distant. All Lily could focus on was her arm, as blood dripped down to her elbow, forming a pool on the ground. Her breath came in ragged gasps. She'd never had so much physical pain.

Rosa just stepped back, cruelly inspecting her handy work while tears spilled from Lily's eyes onto her cheeks. "What is wrong with you?" she croaked through gritted teeth.

Sarah Jane pushed past Rosa and gently caught the wounded arm in her grip. Her voice came in a whisper. "I'm still getting a handle on how to do this, and my friend needs healing. Help me."

Was that a prayer?

The pain coursed through Lily's arm, even with the light touch from Sarah Jane. Her fingers didn't want to move and her hand hung limp.

A strange sensation bloomed in her injured arm. It felt like tiny worms crawling around under her skin. Then a crescendo of relief surged within, and a tremor shook her body. Holding her arm in front of her, she wiggled the fingers. Her hand worked, her skin had stitched back together, and the bone felt whole. The pain was gone.

Sarah Jane had healed the gruesome injury.

Lily gave her a tight hug. "Oh, Sarah Jane! Thank you so much. That was … That was incredible."

She pulled away and wiped her eyes. The landing was empty. Where had that heartless Rosa gone? The door they waited by was open. Only one way to go to find out. She'd certainly tell Simon of the horrible thing Rosa had done.

Chapter Forty-Six

Lily and Sarah Jane climbed out through the rear doorway and onto the roof, a wide expanse given the large size of the building.

Lily spotted a couple of large vents and a large antenna. Toward the front of the building sat a huge, black, ball-like structure with strips of gold inlaid across its surface. A beautiful design. It drew Lily to it, like it was made for her.

Simon stood by the oversized metal basketball, flanked by Rosa, Kelsey, and another guy that she'd seen at some of the conference events. Must be one of the staff. Rosa argued with Simon until he put his hand on her shoulder. Her agitated gestures stopped, and she quietly took a couple of steps aside.

Simon looked up and spotted them. "Girls, I'm glad you made it up. Come over here. I need to show you something very cool."

Lily marched over with Sarah Jane trailing a step behind. Lily thrust a finger at Rosa.

"She just broke my wrist! She grabbed me around my brace-let and squeezed until it crushed my arm. The bracelet fell off, ruined." She held her arm out for a demonstration. "Thankfully Sarah Jane was able to heal me. Rosa needs to be kicked out of here. She's nothing but a monster."

Rosa stood serenely, without any sass or sarcasm. Lily expected her to come after her either verbally or physically. *Weird*.

Simon came over and hooked his arm around Lily's shoulders, and a thrill shot through her body, followed by a strange calm. The horrid injury she'd endured wasn't such a big deal anymore. She'd been healed, right?

"I'm sorry about that. Rosa seems to have quite a temper. We'll need to work on that." He looked at Sarah Jane. "Thank you for healing her. I knew your power was amazing."

Sarah Jane looked at the ground focusing all her attention on her shoes. Her cheeks flushed bright red.

Simon led Lily around the shiny orb. "Now I've got something very important for you to do. Can you help me with it?"

His dark eyes pleaded with hers. If she kept getting looks like that, she'd do whatever he needed. "I'll do my best."

He drew her over to the chair. "We're working on a new energy system. If we can use alternate energy sources to power Alturas as a proof of concept, we can work on extending it throughout the country. We discovered a new way to collect solar energy. Our investors need a better experiment to prove it works."

Lily pushed her hair out of her face. "I could use my power to be your light source."

His hand cupped her chin ever so carefully. "Brilliant girl. I knew I could count on you for help. Now, you'll sit here in this special amplifier chair. It will take in your light and run it into the sphere to process it. But before you say yes, I need you to know that it may be uncomfortable. It could hurt a lot."

She blinked at him.

Simon held his forehead, shaking it. "You know, I shouldn't ask. It's too much to put you in such a position."

She glimpsed Sarah Jane in her peripheral vision. "I can take pain. And we've got Sarah Jane here if something happens. She can heal me."

Sarah Jane's eyes grew huge at the suggestion, but she nodded after a moment. "I think I'm getting the hang of this. I'll be here for you."

Lily looked down at the chair again. A headgear apparatus like the Focuser helmets from yesterday sat on the cushion. Some gauntlets with wiring led to a metal post connected to the base of the sphere.

Not the most comfortable setup. Still, she could do this. It was the least she could do after all Alturas and Simon had done for her.

"Okay, Simon. I'm ready."

Chapter Forty-Seven

Demarcus and Harry entered the campus and made their way toward the far end. It was quiet up front. Usually more workers were milling about the front buildings. The cafeteria had gone silent, too. Demarcus ducked over to the door to throw away his soda.

Yeah, no one was in there. Maybe someone had called an all-hands meeting for everyone.

They passed Redwood Hall and realized where everyone had gone. A crowd of people surrounded Simon's headquarters. It looked like staff and attendees. He recognized Jim and Bruce in the front of the mass of people.

Harry pointed at the crowd. "Okay, this is weird. Aren't the other kids supposed to be in their own focus groups in Albert Hall? What's going on there? Something just doesn't seem right, man."

Harry's worried face spoke volumes. Demarcus felt his heart racing. A sense of foreboding once again snaked its way through his body.

Simon pulled out a gummy bear. Orange. That didn't bode well. He popped it in his mouth and pulled out another one. He sighed in relief at the green candy. Green was his sign of success.

Otto and Kelsey finished with connecting the headset to Lily along with the gloves, then joined him. Rosa stayed farther back, his muscle in case anyone tried to interfere. Rosa was a wild spirit, so broken that he couldn't be confident of full control. Thankfully the bracelet did its trick, pushing his influence directly to her.

"Are you ready, Lily?"

She peeked up at him, her blue eyes radiant in the sun. Such a shame if she was lost. He'd do what he could to salvage her. "I think so. How long will this take?"

"I'm not sure. It might take fifteen minutes to reach full capacity. We'll ramp it up slowly and see how it goes." Sympathetic lies were so much more soothing than the cold truth. Always making people know you cared was such a useful tool in his arsenal.

"Are we ready?" he asked.

Lily nodded, and his staffers double-checked things. Otto signaled thumbs up at the laptop. His job would be to direct the connections to the fiber optic bank. Kelsey monitored everything else on the rooftop.

Sarah Jane stood to the side, eyes wide. As he went to put his hands on the control plates for the Source, he noticed her bracelet was off. When had she done that?

Then his skin made contact.

The Source didn't slowly hum as it normally did. With Lily connected, it roared to life. Light danced beneath each of the gold strips, so brightly that they sparkled, even in the afternoon sun. The effect was instantaneous. He could feel the power drawing from him and magnifying a hundredfold already.

Lily whimpered in front of him, her breath coming in short gulps. "Simon, this really hurts. It's like it is sucking everything out of me. I don't know how long I can do it." She groaned and arched her back against the chair.

It wasn't going to work without sacrifice. He felt a pang of guilt, but to stop now would invite terror from his Master. Simon couldn't face that, and who knows what the Master would do to Lily. "You can do it. It will only be a few more minutes."

Truth was, Simon didn't feel great either. The heat generated by the Source felt like it would fuse him to the machine.

He could overcome pain.

Lily shrieked and her body contorted in the chair. The blood-curdling sound shocked his ears. This wasn't what he expected. Sarah Jane ran up to him. "You're hurting her! Turn it off!"

"I can't. I'm sure it'll clear soon."

Demarcus's phone rang, and the screen read "John."

"Hello?"

"Demarcus? What is happening?"

"There's a crowd of people surrounding Simon's headquarters. The campus seems deserted. We're heading over there. I don't like what I'm feeling, John. It's like a sense of warning, or danger."

"This is part of walking in your gift by the power of the Spirit. God knows all, and He warns His servants."

"Kinda like a holy spider-sense?"

Harry flashed him a strange look. "What are you talking about, John?"

John's words came through garbled.

"Can you repeat that?" Demarcus heard some scuffling, and then their mentor came through clear.

"I know not what spiders have to do with anything. I climbed up on the table here at In-N-Out Burger. A very intense light is emitting from the top of that building. I think they have Lily up there using her power for something. I don't know what for sure, but it is not good. You need to get in there and rescue her."

"What would they use her power for?"

John gasped. "Of course! Lily was dancing with the light last night! Her gift could power the device on the blueprints. She was the objective for Simon's machine."

Shouts sounded on the other side of the line. Demarcus asked, "John, what's going on?"

"I must call you back. It seems the manager does not wish me to remain up here. Call me when you get her."

Demarcus turned to his friend. Harry had his own cell out, his face blanching. "It's Sarah Jane. She said they've hooked Lily up to some machine for her light powers and it's hurting her."

Chapter Forty-Eight

Demarcus pointed toward the light. "I'm going to rush ahead and see if I can get her. I'll meet you there as soon as you can arrive."

Before Harry could respond, Demarcus took off. It felt good to accelerate. He raced past a few stragglers and closed the distance to the headquarters. His feet dug into the grass as he skidded to a stop, sending the scent of fresh earth into the air.

The youths and staff encircled the building. They acted like they were in conversation, yet they formed a perfect human wall in front of the doors. Demarcus took off and sprinted around the exterior of the building in a couple of seconds. No opening.

He jogged up to the front of the building. "Hey guys, I need to get in. I'm supposed to see Simon right now."

A few heads swiveled his way, each person with a blank stare in his or her eyes. "Simon is not to be disturbed. We are here to protect Simon."

A scream sounded from above. Demarcus glanced up to see a burst of light from the rooftop. The intensity burned his eyes, and when he looked away, bright streaks blurred his vision for a moment. More shrieks. He heard Sarah Jane yelling, "Stop!" and a primal wail carrying through the air.

He couldn't play nice this time. "Look out, gang, I've got to get through." Demarcus tried to push between the weakest link, a short girl and a pudgy guy with glasses. They resisted, and Demarcus found himself caught from behind. Hands clawed at his arms and torso and threw him to the ground.

He bounced up and tried to cut through the gap they'd created, but the crush of people pushed together and stopped him again.

"Let me through. Someone's getting hurt up there, and I need to help them!" Demarcus took a few steps back. If he had a running start, it would be like Red Rover in kindergarten. Oh yeah, he was coming through.

He pumped his legs and collided with the arms of the smallest people he could see. The two he hit collapsed, but he was slowed enough that the others seized his arms and legs before he could get moving. He tried to yank free, wrestling against the people next to him. Anytime he freed himself from one grip, another hand took its place.

Another screech sounded from above. Demarcus tumbled to the ground, his body smashed by the sheer number of people on him. The side of his face pressed into the grass, and pain shot through his head. He tried to call for help, but all the air squeezed out of his lungs.

He couldn't breathe.

Simon bore down, willing the process to speed up. Maybe he could at least lessen Lily's suffering by making it go faster.

The sensation jerked to a stop, and his head swam with the abrupt change.

Sarah Jane freed Lily from the helmet and pulled her up. She'd yanked his power source out of the chair.

"Get her in the chair!" Simon yelled.

"*No*. You're hurting her. I won't let you do this anymore." She put her hand on Lily's forehead and furrowed her brow, apparently trying to heal her.

The heat from the panels on the Source fused his skin to the surface. He'd rip the skin off his palms if he tried to move until he gave it the one-minute cool-off. Time for Plan B.

He looked behind his shoulder and flicked his head forward.

Sarah Jane hooked Lily's shoulder around her neck and started helping her toward the door. Before they could get far, Rosa rushed up to them.

She knocked Sarah Jane sprawling and picked Lily up by the waist, setting her down in the chair. Simon motioned with his eyes for Kelsey to redo the set-up for the Source.

Then it all went haywire.

He watched, helpless to physically intervene, as Sarah Jane jumped up and slapped Rosa across the cheek. "Stop it! You're going to kill her."

Rosa growled a curse and snagged Sarah Jane by her neck. She scratched at Rosa's arms as her feet lifted off the ground, kicking furiously. Her face turned purple, only hoarse croaks leaving her mouth.

Lily screamed, terror lacing her voice.

Simon's focus was still recovering. He tried to override Rosa's primal rage. "Put her down. Just knock her out or something. There's no reason to go crazy. Rosa!"

Simon continued to yell as Rosa threw Sarah Jane over the edge of the roof.

Chapter Forty-Nine

Demarcus felt a release of pressure just as the edges of his vision started to darken. Before they could get another grip, he scrambled up on all fours and rolled out of the way, bowling one person over as he tumbled.

He shook the cobwebs from his head and moved into a crouch position, at the ready like a sprinter. Just then Harry came running past him, a terrified sound coming from his mouth, his hands reaching out.

Demarcus turned to see the trajectory of Harry's gaze and saw a body land to the side of the crowd, a sickening thump announcing its impact.

He recognized her—it was Sarah Jane.

"No!" His own voice cried out in unison with his friend's. Demarcus blasted forward, arriving at her side in a flash.

Her arm bent in an unnatural position behind her. Blood trickled from the corner of her mouth. She struggled to take a breath.

"Don't worry," Demarcus said. "Harry and I are here. We're going to get help."

Harry slid down on his knees next to her as well.

Sarah Jane coughed, spitting out more blood. "Now I know why I didn't see anything … with the Focuser. I had … no potential."

Harry shook, tears streaming down his face. "No, no, no. We can get help. You … can you heal yourself? Come on, Sarah Jane. You can do it."

Her eyelids fluttered. "Save Lily. They're … gonna kill her."

Sarah Jane's eyes closed, her body stilled. Her head turned to the side.

Demarcus slumped in shock. How could this happen? They had powers. God was with them, according to John. Something tickled his cheek. His hand swiped at his face and came away damp with tears.

Harry crumpled on the ground next to her, sobbing.

A streak of illumination cascaded from the roof. Lily. Sarah Jane had just died trying to help her, he was sure of it. He surveyed the human shield around the building. Still nowhere for him to go. There was only one chance.

He shook Harry by the shoulders. "Dude, get a hold of yourself. We can't help Sarah Jane, but Lily is trapped up there, and it looks like they're doing something horrible to her." A cry rang out from above, confirming his suspicion. "You're her only chance. All these peeps are Simon's zombies, and I can't get through. You can teleport up there."

Harry moaned and rocked his head back and forth. "I can't. I don't know how."

What could Demarcus do? Only one thing came to mind.

He laid his hand on Harry's forehead and prayed. "Lord, we need your strength and grace. Harry needs your empowering to save our friend. You gave this to him, now please help him use it."

Demarcus pulled Harry's head up and fixed him with a gaze. His red, swollen eyes matched his hair color. "Go get her. We'll save her and stop Simon from doing this to anyone else. And take these." He slipped his favorite shades into Harry's hand.

Harry stood up and bent his legs at the knees. He stared up at the roof and a tremble washed over him. "C'mon man. You got this," Harry muttered.

Nothing happened.

The sky grew brighter, despite the midday sun. Another scream echoed from above. Demarcus scanned the surroundings, trying to find some way to get pass the human barrier.

Harry closed his eyes and jumped. Still nothing.

How were they going to do anything? Demarcus had one fleeting thought. He dashed away.

A scared voice called after him. "Where are you going?"

Demarcus stopped one hundred yards away and locked eyes with Harry. This had better work, or they would both be in trouble.

Demarcus pumped his legs into the ground, pistons that shot him forward. Straight towards Harry.

With his enhanced reflexes, Demarcus could make out Harry's mouth gaping at his approach.

Demarcus braced for impact. Nothing was going to happen.

The atmosphere warped for a moment and Harry disappeared.

Chapter Fifty

Lily didn't know what made her cry out more: Sarah Jane's fall from the roof or the pain searing every fiber in her body. Light poured out uncontrollably as the awful machine sucked her dry, pulling the rays from her. Rosa stood in front of her, a leer on her face. Lily, in a moment of coherence, pictured a laser shooting from her finger and frying the witch's face off.

She thrashed her body to and fro, but Kelsey had hooked a belt across her lap. It didn't matter; with the machine engaged, her hands were stuck in place so she couldn't free herself anyway.

Simon had cussed out Rosa when she chucked Sarah Jane over the edge, yet he remained indifferent to Lily's suffering. No matter how much she pleaded with him, she realized no relief was coming.

Her heart thudded against her chest, about ready to pound out of her ribcage. Death would be a relief from the torture she fought at this point.

Before another thought came to her, Harry appeared beside her, wearing Demarcus's fancy sunglasses.

How did that happen?

She wanted to warn him about the danger. Before she could, he grabbed her arm. She felt a quick shake through his fingers, and then the pain came to a sudden end.

Lily grabbed for anything to steady her spinning head. She stumbled onto the grass, and her insides threatened to find the outside. *What just happened?*

Harry and Demarcus leaned over her. "Are you all right?"

"Where am I?" Her whole body buzzed from the light Simon had just sucked out of her.

The two guys pulled her to her feet and hugged her. Demarcus whispered in her ear. "We got you down on the ground. But we're so, so sorry. We ... couldn't save Sarah Jane."

Shock reverberated throughout her bones. Sarah Jane had died trying to save her.

A shout came from the roof. They all looked up to see Simon pointing down at them. "Get those three and bring them to me now!"

The mass of people around the building started toward them, encircling them and cutting off their escape. Lily saw Missy in the crowd reaching out, a blank look in her eyes. Rival or not, something had overtaken Missy's mind.

Demarcus looked around frantically. "If I take Lily, I can outrun them. Harry, can you teleport out of here?"

He nodded. "I think so."

Lily couldn't keep up with everything. "Wait a minute—that's your ability? You can teleport?"

"Yep. But we should go now."

"No. We're not going to get away from the crowd, and we have to stop Simon. He's not going to let us go. Can you get us back up there?"

Harry glanced at the swarm about to overtake them. "I don't know. I've only done it once before."

Demarcus took a hold of his arm. "Now's a good time to try it, I'd say."

Harry pulled Lily close, and another faint shake vibrated through her. Hands reached out for them. Too late to escape.

Chapter Fifty-One

Lily stumbled again upon landing. *That is the freakiest trip ever.* Demarcus wavered and held his stomach, while Harry grinned. *What made him smile at a time like this? His power?* The horrid machine droned with an irritating sound, as if it ran slightly out of gear.

Simon whirled around at their presence.

"You three are going to ruin everything. You've got one chance to survive. Lily, connect to the Source, and I'll let your friends live."

Lily wanted to rip the eyes out of his head. "You killed Sarah Jane. There's no way I'm getting back in that thing. Pull the plug, now!"

Simon glared at them. "I want you all to lie down on the ground and stay there."

A force pulled at her mind. She really wanted to comply—the power that tugged at her was strong and hard to resist. Her knees almost buckled. The image of Sarah Jane in terror as she fell dissipated the mental suggestion.

Tendrils of black radiated from Simon out toward her. The dark also framed Rosa, and pulses from Simon continued to enshroud her.

Is that what the black she'd been seeing was? Evil? People controlled by Simon?

"No, Simon. You can't control us anymore. Not after what just happened. What was so important about that stupid ball that you strapped me to a torture device?"

Simon pleaded with them. "I didn't *want* her to die, and I didn't mean to do that to you. But with this amplifier, my gift will spread around the globe, carried along Alturas's fiber optic cables by your light. With that wave carrying it, Alturas can influence the world. If we're going to change things, that's how it's going to happen. I need your help, Lily."

Demarcus whispered to her. "Don't listen to him. I'll take him out."

She put a hand on his chest shaking her head. "No, he's mine."

"If I can't convince you to help me … Rosa, bring her to me."

Rosa started forward, a sneer plastered across her mug. Lily took a reflexive step backwards. Demarcus zipped behind Rosa and caught her arms behind her. She laughed as she broke his grip and swung him across the roof. He tumbled along the rooftop and lay sprawled out on the cement.

A fire burned behind Lily's eyes, and the image of Sarah Jane plunging over the edge fueled it. She'd regret what she did.

Lily focused all her anger into a ball of rage that formed inside of her. The force of her emotions shook her body. This girl thought she was tough? She had to get past Lily first.

She thrust her arms out toward her assailant, and a beam of photonic energy erupted from her palms. It slammed into Rosa's torso and knocked her back where she hit the lip of the roof, sending her tumbling over the edge. A screech echoed with her fall until it went silent.

Lily's hands burned from the release of energy from her body. She shook them out, trying to get feeling to return to her fingers. What did she just do? A quiver overtook her muscles.

Did she just kill Rosa?

To her left, Otto and Kelsey fled to the stairwell. Demarcus had recovered and joined Harry in flanking her. They looked as stunned as she about what had just occurred.

It was just them and Simon now.

Simon's face softened. "Look, you don't understand. The world needs order. You three know how chaotic it is out there. You've all suffered from it. Lily, how much have you suffered through the death of your mother? Or because of what happened to your brother?

"Our plan was to bring a framework to help the youth rise up and change things. I want to prevent tragedies like what happened to you from ever happening again. We can still do it. Lily, if you can control your power like that, the Source doesn't have to pull it out of you. You can infuse it with the light needed to shuttle the message throughout the world. You can do this. It's in your hands."

Fatigue crept into Lily. She didn't know the limits of her power, not to mention the physical strain and emotional toll. But she couldn't stop now. How *dare* he bring her mother into this?

Still, was there truth in what he said? His suggestions pulled at her mental resistance, probing for weak points.

The abject terror in Sarah Jane's eyes stood as the barrier preventing him from taking control.

"No, Simon. I'm not doing this. You want to control things. You want to bend it to your will. That's not life worth living. We have to be free, and I'm going to make sure that there's nothing left of this Source."

Chapter Fifty-Two

Everything crumbled in an instant. Simon stared at Lily, her skin alight with an eerie glow, wondering how it all went wrong. She'd been there in the Source, and the stream of control was propagating out into the columns. Then she disappeared. When he thought the people under his control had them down on the ground, she appeared again with the two boys.

Of course. Harry's unknown power. He could teleport. Why had Simon not been able to figure that out?

Now it was a standoff. He stood alone against three gifted teens. If he could get his power through to her subconscious, maybe he had a chance. Since Rosa had ruined Lily's bracelet, it had to be through direct contact.

At this moment, Lily had to be managed carefully. The way she'd created a solid photonic beam to blast Rosa off the roof was incredible. She could burn a hole through him in an instant if she wanted.

But he had to try. The Master was waiting.

"Lily, I was wrong to force you into this. And you have to believe me; I never wanted Rosa to hurt Sarah Jane. She was too hard to control. That's why I need your help. The power of light will amplify the signal and speed it to every corner of the world. We can bring peace and comfort to people."

He thought about her file, grasping for any scrap of information that could keep this going. "You didn't have that when your mother and brother died. Your father didn't know how to comfort you. That's part of my gift. I can feel your needs and show you how to get where you need to be. Let me help you." He took a cautious step forward. "Come to me, and I'll guide you through this."

Simon had never poured out so much force into his influence before. He flooded the teens with suggestion. Sweat dripped from his brow and his stomach churned. His opponents held their ground, wary of him. He split his commands toward the trio. He needed the boys to stay back, and Lily to relent.

Another step. If he could get his hand on her, the direct contact should be able to override her anger at Sarah Jane's death.

Lily frowned and looked at Demarcus. Simon crept closer. One more step and he'd have her. His hand reached out.

"Let's work together to change this world for the better."

Lily shivered, and he felt her mental resistance buckle for a moment. Now was his chance. He caught her arm. She froze as his thoughts invaded her nerves, streaming calm through her body.

Something slammed into him, knocking him onto the ground next to the Source. When he looked up again, Demarcus and Lily stood several feet away. The speedster. Of course.

Demarcus stared him down. "Hands off, jerk."

Why wasn't his power working on Demarcus or Harry?

He glanced at Harry and noticed something affixed behind his ear. A Nullifier.

John …

Lily set her feet and pointed something at him. Simon raised his hands in submission. He couldn't catch her now.

"I think I know how to get to you." She called over her shoulder, "Boys, you might want to cover your eyes." Her hands trembled, and Simon noticed a silver tube sticking out from her grasp. The laser pointer from his rally yesterday. She caught it?

Simon's arms reflexively lifted to protect his face and eyes. He feared the luminosity she could muster.

Nothing happened. He dropped his hands and saw a concentrated beam of light streaking past him.

Burning into the Source.

No! Take my life. Anything but that!

Simon ran for the orb.

He moved to throw his body in the way when a small trail of smoke appeared. The shell cracked, and an explosion lifted him off the roof. Fiery pain scorched his face as he flew through the sky.

Once he hit the dirt, his suffering would end. He would finally escape the torment of his Master.

Instead of plowing into the grass or crunching against cement, a pair of arms enveloped him. How did that happen? He tried to open his eyes, except they wouldn't obey.

Wait. The eyelids moved. He just couldn't see.

As he sat cradled in his savior's arms, pain racking his body, a familiar voice whispered to him.

"Where should I take you, Señor?"

Chapter Fifty-Three

Demarcus dove to the cement, his arms above his head. Even under cover, the brightness that burst overhead shone through his eyelids. The roof shook with the explosion.

Well, that's it. We're going down in a blaze of glory. Literally.

His ears rang when the blast stopped. Fiery bits of debris rained down on him. He looked around. At least the roof hadn't collapsed.

A tremor vibrated under him. Okay, it hadn't collapsed *yet*.

He lifted his head, but the brightness prevented him from opening his eyes. "Harry? Lily? Are you okay?"

Harry groaned, and it sounded close by. Demarcus shuffled on his knees, feeling in front of him. A couple of feet away his fingers found a head of spiky hair. The head shifted under his hand. All right, Harry was alive.

"Lily!"

"I'm here," came an ethereal whisper.

Where was she? The sky blazed a brilliant white that kept him from peeking out. Too bad he'd handed off his shades to Harry.

Demarcus groped around. A piece of rubble burned his hand. He dropped the hot scrap and shook his hand out, then he sucked on his fingers for some quick relief. Reaching out again, he felt a cool plastic strip. His glasses.

Demarcus thrust them on and carefully opened his eyes. Still uncomfortably bright, but he could make out a few outlines. A nexus of radiation defied direct observation. He assumed the center of illumination was the Source burning up. He saw a crater in the roof where the circular object had been. No, the epicenter of the light had to be Lily.

He slowly stood up and pushed into the dazzling flash. "Lily, Simon's gone. The Source is destroyed. You can turn it off now."

Her voice was faint. "I can't control it. It's streaming out of me. Leave me. I'm going to burn up here. It's over."

The ground shifted again. This roof wasn't going to last much longer. "No, Lily. We won't leave you. Come on. I can't see you, so I need you to come to me. I'll get you out of here."

Her words dripped with regret. "I killed two people. I'm as bad as Simon. I'm not worth saving. I can control light, but everything in my life turns to darkness."

Demarcus's skin heated up. He was getting a sunburn just standing there. Demarcus pushed forward, even with the air sizzling ahead of him.

How could he reach her? It was too much. She needed someone to stand with her. Otherwise she'd burn up and take the rest of them with her. *Lord, give me strength to help her. Be with her. Show her your true light.*

The brightness shimmered, and he saw a corona around Lily. Her arms were outstretched, and her hair fluttered around her. Then a second form materialized, opened his arms, and embraced Lily. His hair and clothes shone with a light separate from Lily's.

Is that who I think it is?

The brilliance intensified one last time, forcing Demarcus to protect his eyes again. Then it slowly faded, and one figure stood wavering in front of him.

Lily. She started to slump.

He dashed over and caught her. There was no one else on the roof aside from Harry, who stood up, swaying on his feet, a few yards away.

Slumping to the ground for a moment, he caught his breath. What just happened? Despite the heat from the Source's explosion, a chill rippled down him. He'd encountered something holy today. A whispered prayer of thanks escaped his lips.

A noise drew his attention back to their immediate circumstances. Demarcus peered over the edge of the hole in the roof where the Source had been. A pile of rubble lay strewn on the floor below. Then a new piece fell from the edge and shattered on impact. His weight shifted as cracks spread throughout the cement beneath their feet.

He called out, "We've got to get out of here, now! Take Lily and get her safe." Demarcus handed her over to Harry. She barely held her own weight, and she was too dazed to respond.

"What are you going to do?"

"This roof is going to collapse, and I need to make sure there's no one else in here. That's what I can do. Now go!"

The two of them blinked away, then Demarcus sprinted to the stairwell and slid on the handrails to the next floor. He raced down the hallway, yelling out a warning for anyone to evacuate. Where were the two assistants?

He didn't move as fast with the lateral movement of checking doors and rooms. He peeked into every open door to confirm no one else was inside.

He cleared the third floor as best as he could tell. Just as he hit the stairs, the far end collapsed through to the next level. He sped down to the next level to see if anyone was hurt there. A tall man with a goatee scrambled out of the dust cloud that filtered through the air.

"Kelsey's caught. I can't get her out!" he called.

The soot choked Demarcus's throat. He coughed, but he reached the pile. On the far side a woman lay with her leg trapped under a large piece of scrap.

"Let's get her out." A little shake trembled under his feet. He guessed what that meant. "We've got to hurry."

The two of them tossed aside chunks of wood and concrete. His hands bled from various scrapes from the debris. Another shudder. How long until they could slide Kelsey out?

They reached the one large beam that directly pinned her legs. With a loud grunt, they dislodged the wood and freed her leg. Demarcus turned to the other guy. "Get out of here. I'll get her. I think this whole building is about to crumble."

The dude didn't need convincing, and he scrambled around the pile to the hallway. Demarcus finished freeing Kelsey and slung her over his shoulder. The floor shifted, and he barely jumped out of the way when a large chunk slid down into another hole that caved in from the weight.

They cleared the hallway. He had to descend the stairs slowly with the unbalanced load he carried. Kelsey mumbled something incoherent on the way down. He hit the main floor and pivoted to race out the front.

The pile of rubble blocked the access.

Kelsey lifted her head. "Go to the left. I can get us out."

Before Demarcus turned, the pillars out front tumbled into bits. The whole front of the house was going down.

He cut left and dashed into an unassuming little office that only had small windows that wouldn't fit either of them.

"Get me to the panel." Kelsey's voice croaked.

Demarcus whirled. A control panel was built into the wall next to the door. He positioned Kelsey and she tapped in a code.

A filing cabinet slid to the side, revealing a gap in the floor.

"Simon liked to have fun. It's a slide. Let's go."

Demarcus set her on the slide and she disappeared into the darkness. More vibrations ratcheted through the building. Time to scram. He dropped in and coasted down the ramp, running into Kelsey at the bottom.

"Where does this go?"

She held her ankle. Still she managed a grimacing smile. "Wait until you see this."

Chapter Fifty-Four

Lily tottered on the grass after Harry teleported them down and started shouting for people to run. It seemed like everyone at the conference had encircled the building. They all looked confused, and many of them held their heads as if battling headaches. The sounds of wood snapping and concrete crumbling spurred them on, and the crowd started to flee.

The only thing Lily could do was slump to the ground. The effort of holding her head up almost proved too much. Forget about standing or walking at this point. Harry came over to check on her.

A thought jolted her system. "Where's Demarcus?"

"He went through the building to warn people to get out. Otherwise I would've brought him along."

She searched the building for any clues. Hunks of stone fell off the front pillars and crashed onto the patio below. "Can you go in and check for him?"

He leaned over, hands on his knees. "I don't know how much more I can do. I can try though."

Before Harry could try, the pillars began collapsing Shards of stone shattered and the central fiber optic cables splayed out. The roof crushed through the remaining supports, and the whole front of the building toppled onto the ground.

Harry slumped on the lawn next to her. "Holy cow!"

A fine cloud of particles settled on all of the onlookers marveling at the collapse. Most of the teenagers had their phones out recording all of the proceedings.

Ironically, they were probably using Flare to document the demise of Alturas.

A voice called out from within the settling dust. "Harry? Demarcus? Are you out there?" Lily recognized the voice.

The old man.

John appeared through the grit, carrying someone in his arms. Sarah Jane.

Lily scrambled up and shuffled over to him. Sarah Jane had died trying to save her. Why did this have to happen?

John set the girl down on the grass as Lily came up to them. Harry dropped next to her, and his tears formed a muddy trail down his cheeks.

"Sarah Jane, thank you." Lily's voice croaked in a whisper. Shock constricted her throat.

John cradled Sarah Jane's head and spoke words low and fast in a language Lily couldn't understand.

Lily tore a scrap from the sleeve of her shirt and dabbed at the dried blood on Sarah Jane's chin. The gesture was pointless, but Lily wanted, no, she needed to do something for her.

Sarah Jane's mouth opened and she sucked in a gulp of air.

What?

Sarah Jane coughed and groaned, wriggling a little on the ground. She didn't regain consciousness, but her chest moved up and down in regular intervals.

Harry cried next to her. "What—she was dead! I saw her slip away!"

John put a hand on the boy's knee. "The Lord is gracious. He let her live."

What the—? Is this even real? Lily didn't know what to think. Her mind had completely numbed after the last couple of hours. One thought forced through her muddled brain.

"Has anyone seen Demarcus?"

John shook his head and started scanning the crowd.

Harry stood up and called, "Demarcus?"

"You lookin' for me, bro?"

Demarcus approached from behind them with Kelsey leaning on him for support. Her ankle was bent at a weird angle. They stopped and he helped Kelsey to the ground so she could take the weight off of it.

Lily clambered over to him and wrapped her arms around his neck. "You're okay!"

"So are you. I had to make sure that no one else was going to die today in that building. Another guy and I pulled her out."

She pointed down to where Sarah Jane lay. John sat on the ground next to her, still stroking her hair, softly speaking comforting words. "You're not the only hero today," she said. "Look."

Demarcus's mouth opened wide in shock. "What? She wasn't breathing. We saw her fall. We saw her die."

Lily knelt down next to Sarah Jane. Tears dropped onto her friend's face. She looked up at John. "Apparently, I was wrong about you. Really wrong." She paused to control a sob. "I'm so sorry for running away. I went right into Simon's trap, and it almost cost us everything."

John gave her a warm smile. "Dear child, it was a powerful deception. Look at all of these other people drawn in. It was not a failure on your part. In my opinion, you overcame the odds smashingly." He thumbed behind him to the ruined hulk of a building.

Sirens sounded in the distance. The light show and demolition must have caught the attention of the authorities.

"Did anyone see what happened to Simon? Or Rosa?"

John cleared his throat. "I saw a body tumble off the building over there." He pointed to the far side from where they sat. "But when I arrived, there was only a body-sized crater. Then I circled the perimeter and found Sarah Jane."

Lily hoped they hadn't died. But the thought of them still out there unsettled her.

Demarcus chuckled. "Harry and I were too busy saving you. You could've whipped out that laser sooner, ya know." He winked at her. "But, I'm glad you didn't. That was amazing to watch."

"You moved so fast. I thought Simon had me for a second there. His mind voodoo is hard to clear out of your head."

Harry nudged Demarcus. "Do you think you had a little help there?"

Demarcus snickered. "Naw, I had it under control."

Lily couldn't believe all that had changed in her life in just three days. She'd discovered an amazing gift, and she learned she wasn't alone. What did all this mean? So many questions. Time to get a few answers.

"John, it seemed like you expected this. How could someone really see all of this coming?"

"Haven't you heard of prophecy?" His bushy eyebrows raised.

She cocked her head to the side. "You mean someone can tell the future?"

"Do you really doubt it after today?"

He had her there. "Fair enough. But where did these gifts come from?"

Sarah Jane started to stir. "What happened? I feel like I got run over by a semi."

She tried to sit up. John put a calming hand on her shoulder. "Just rest, child. I was just going to tell Lily a story about a carpenter and his friends from a long time ago. And how you were made for such a time as this."

Epilogue

Adeniji Okeofor stepped into his private chamber. It was time to confer with the rest of the Archai. The Four had to address the failure of their apprentice and deal with the new threat that had arisen over the last few days.

The reflective surfaces glowed with a faint green hue. Adeniji took his seat, legs crossed, on the ancient stone passed down to him from his predecessor on the Four. A spasm shot through his body, the familiar sensation that occurred every time he used the portal. He loosed his tongue and a torrent of words formed the chant that would link them together.

His mind cleared with the repetition of the words. Soon a darkened skyscape was all that remained, with streaks of light occasionally breaking the oppressive blackness.

As he remained in this state, other forms began to emerge, vapors assembling into familiar forms. Violette Dupris materialized on his left. The French woman's visage rippled, her eyes only pale orbs. The same as he must look to her.

The youngest and most recent member, Cezar Pereira, arrived next. The youngest and most recent member to be included. His ambition knew no limit, and Adeniji both appreciated the power the Brazilian brought into the Archai via the Four and was wary of the incessant hunger that he displayed.

Where was Fen? The enigmatic Chinese woman represented the most mysterious of the Four. Oh, there she was. Her presence faded in to the right of him. He could never sense her presence, which always disconcerted him.

"Greetings, chosen ones. I come to you with disappointing news. Our vessel in San Francisco has failed. The Alturas project is over."

"But he is not dead. We have not felt him torn away from the mortal veil." Fen remained the most sensitive to the tethers holding all of their thralls to this side of the divide.

Adeniji waved a dismissive hand. "That is of no consequence now. The Archai must move on, and they need to know what we Four have in mind."

A chuckle escaped the lips of Cezar. "Simple. We remove the foes who stopped us this time, and we reset for another attempt."

Impulsive, as usual. "Violette, you have a reply?"

"*Oui*. We have bigger problems than a few teenagers, even if they have supernatural gifts. That can be countered. In fact, I am working on that right now. However, our adversary has placed a major piece in play against us. If we are to succeed, removing him is the key."

The chamber flashed with images of an old man, worn, yet with a vitality that was outside the natural realm. The strong impression gripped Adeniji that this man would be their undoing, if not dealt with swiftly.

"Do we concur? This man is priority?"

The three other apparitions nodded in unison.

"Then do we have a plan?"

Cezar raised his head. "I have a servant that is prepared to do whatever it takes to make it on the Archai. He is ready to serve us unto death."

Silence held in the air. Fen breathed a reply. "We have many under our sway who would do this. What makes your puppet different?"

"I have already dispatched him to Babylon. He is journeying there as we speak. I have sent him with the scroll to the sacrifice grounds of the temple."

Even in the ethereal confines of the chamber, the chill from the others in the Four spread amongst his fellows as they considered Cezar's insolence. "Who authorized this? We certainly did not assent to this."

"Must we be paralyzed by indecision? I did not see a reason to wait on one plan. Once the Elder appeared, it seemed best to prepare multiple angles to confront the light." A ghostly smirk spread on his face.

The others gave their mental approval. Violette did so with annoyance. Fen seemed pleased that Cezar had operated so independently. Very well. They had their next step.

They would unleash hell to deal with the emissary from Heaven.

Discussion Questions

1. *Launch* is a work of fiction, but set in a present day world. Did this book seem realistic to you? Why or why not?

2. What did you like best about this book? What did you like least about this book?

3. In the first chapter, Demarcus is checking out his gift of speed and wonders what to do with it. What are your gifts—music, sports, writing, baking, etc.? Do you wonder what to do with your God-given gifts? How do you determine what they are?

4. Demarcus helps the homeless alcoholic by getting him to the hospital, but while there, he's questioned by a police officer and he fudges his answers and takes off to avoid questioning. He even asks for forgiveness as he does it. Do you agree with how he handled things? Why or why not?

5. Lily is dealing with sadness and depression when we first meet her. How have you handled things when you are down? How do you think you could help someone like Lily in your life?

6. Iaonnes (aka John) has seen much in his lifetime. Which individual (grandparent, sibling, mentor) in your life could you interview to learn about their life experiences? When was the last time you did something like this?

7. Simon Mazor has a quirk of ascribing luck to whatever color of gummy bear he pulls out. Do you have any beliefs that influence you? What's a fun quirk or habit that you have?

8. John tells Demarcus and Harry that it is destiny that they have these gifts, that it's part of God's plan. Do you believe we have a destiny, or is it up to us to determine our fate?

9. Demarcus is asked what traits he thinks are most important in a man and woman during his interview at the conference. What do you believe are the most important character traits for a man or a woman to have?

10. Out of all of the "powers" revealed in Launch, which one would you want? Is there a power not mentioned?

11. Simon says when youth are unified they will be a "vanguard for humanity". The Bible speaks of unity for God's people in Psalm 133 and John 17. How do you think Christians can come together and be more unified?

12. John is complimented on how clean his bathrooms gets, and he prays while scrubbing toilets. Do you do all of your work as unto the Lord? Can any job be glorifying to God?

13. Simon has a gift to influence people, even to the point of

mind-control, when he tries his hardest. Who are the people that influence you in life? Do they point you toward good things, or have you allowed negative influencers to have sway over you?

14. Lily points out that the attendees are brought together because they're broken—they've had some kind of trauma in life that has deeply affected them. Have you struggled with a trial or trauma in your life? What have you done to find help or healing for it? Are there things you could still do to get healthy?

15. Flare is the social media the kids used in the book. Social media has become a huge part of our world in just the last decade. What do you think are the benefits of social media? What are the drawbacks?

16. There are a lot of geeky references in the book. Part of the fun writing it was slipping things like that in. What are your favorite pop culture references you found?

17. Both Lily and Demarcus have experiences where they see something miraculous. Have you ever seen something miraculous happen?

18. What do you think of the book's title? How does it relate to the book's contents? What other title might you choose?

19. What was your favorite quote or passage from the book? Who said it?

20. If you were making a movie of this book, who would you cast? Why?

Author Acknowledgments

A book is not written by just one person. Many people contribute to make a manuscript into something worth sending out into the world. I couldn't have done it without the following people.

Jill Williamson—the story would still be a nugget in my noggin if it weren't for our brainstorming session flying back from Indianapolis. Best flight ever.

Ben Wolf—your editing prowess has done it again. Thanks for pushing me to make this better.

Nadine Brandes—thank you for your insight as well.

Lindsay Schlegel—the final touch. You had so many good suggestions to fine tune things.

Becky Dean—my critique partner who gave me so many ideas to get the manuscript into shape and is always there for bouncing around concepts.

My beta readers—Shan Dittemore, Charity Tinnin, Josh Smith, J.J. Johnson. Your time and comments are so appreciated.

Scott and Becky Minor and all the awesome people at Realm Makers. My tribe helps power me along in the journey.

Cap's Chaps—you guys rock. Just do it!

I wouldn't be on this journey without some friends from KFM— Adria, Athena Prime, Vyperhand, Jiara, Delerious Jedi, Rimwalker, and the rest of the crew. May the Force be with you!

Thanks also to Lindsay Franklin, Peter Leavell, Avily Jerome, Kim Vandel, John Otte, Matt Mikalatos, and all those who have given me encouragement along the way.

Little Lamb Books and Rachel Pellegrino—thank you for believing and inviting me into your family.

I want to thank my wonderful wife Beccy for her love, support, and belief. I wouldn't be here without you.

Nathan, Matthew, Caleb, and Micaiah—you help me see the potential of what God has for the future, and I see the heroic in you. Keep up the good fight!

Finally, thank you to Jesus for making the ultimate heroic sacrifice, and the final victory over death.

About the Author

Jason C. Joyner is a physician assistant living in Idaho with his wife, four kids and their black cat named Anakin. A believer in bacon being awesome and a fan of all things Star Wars, he loves the power of stories and believes we are all given gifts to share with the world. Launch, is his debut novel and the first in the Rise of the Anointed trilogy. You can visit him online at www.jasoncjoyner.com.

Launch is also available as an ebook.

RISE OF THE
ANOINTED

BOOK TWO

JASON C. JOYNER

FRACTURES

Demarcus, Lily, Harry,
and Sarah Jane face off against
new threats, including a mercenary
sent by the Archai to destroy them
after Simon Mazor's failure
at the Launch Conference.

The Anointed must decide
whether they are strong enough
to fight together against the Archai's
latest threat or walk away from
their calling and live with the
wounds they each carry.

For all the latest information
regarding Fractures, book 2 in the
Rise of the Anointed series,
visit www.JasonCJoyner.com
or www.LittleLambBooks.com.